Einstein's Cosmic Journey

A biographical fantasy of quantum proportions

By

Walter E. Jacobson, MD

PREFACE

This book is an amalgam of fact and fantasy. Some of the events depicted actually happened. Others were invented. Some of Einstein's spoken words were his own. Others came from my imagination.

Hopefully, the end result is the portrayal of a brilliant, ever-inquiring scientist and a passionate truth seeker committed to the betterment of humanity.

1

The year is 1919. The place is the University of Berlin. Albert Einstein, at 40 years of age, stands at a lecture podium, giving a speech to a room full of physics students. His hair and moustache are jet black. His eyes sparkle with intellect and humanity. He wears a baggy jacket, baggy trousers, and an old, worn pair of shoes, no socks.

"It saddens me that I cannot sing the praises of scientific progress," Einstein begins. "It has brought such little happiness. In war it has enabled men to mutilate one another more efficiently. And in peace it has enslaved man to the machine. If one wants one's life to be useful to mankind, it is not enough that one understand applied science as such. Scientists should direct their efforts toward those discoveries most beneficial to humanity."

Einstein pauses a moment. "Concern for man and his fate must always form the chief interest of all technical endeavors so as to assure that the results of our scientific thinking may be a blessing to mankind, and not a curse. Never forget this in the midst of your diagrams and equations."

Einstein surveys his audience. They are all enthralled by him. "We have time for one more question."

Dozens of students wave their hands frantically at Einstein, each hoping that he will call upon them. After a moment, Einstein points at one student in particular.

"You there."

"What about atomic energy, Professor Einstein? Do you think it will one day be possible to release the awesome amount of energy defined in your equation by bombardment of the atom?"

"An excellent question, young man. One I can assure you I've given considerable thought." He pauses. "Splitting the atom by bombardment is like shooting at birds in the dark, in a region where there are very few birds. To those who look for sources of power in atomic transmutations, such expectations are an absurd waste of time."

2

The year is 1955. The place is Princeton, New Jersey. It's an average day. An average middle-class suburban neighborhood. Birds chirp idyllically. Dogs playfully bark as they scamper in their yards. Children ride bicycles, play hopscotch and jump rope.

And then, without the least bit of warning, a burst of blinding light! It's an atomic bomb explosion!

A huge, black, hideous mushroom cloud expands upwards, engulfing the sky. A maelstrom of black, atomic dust swirls and howls furiously.

After a few moments, a tiny figure of a man emerges from the cloud. It's Albert Einstein, now 76-years-old, his hair and moustache now white with age. As the atomic storm continues to rage around him, he stops in his tracks and looks down at the ground. Beneath his feet are the fused, melted, charred flesh and bones of human beings. Victims of the atomic devastation grotesquely littered on the ground as far as the eye can see. Einstein is horrified. He lets out a chilling, heart-wrenching scream.

**

Einstein awakens from his nightmare. His face and body are drenched with sweat. A look of horror, guilt and torment is etched across his features.

3

Helen Dukas, 50-years-old and Einstein's personal secretary and living companion, sits at a breakfast table set for two. Einstein, looking weary and disheveled, shuffles into the room and takes a seat at the table.

"Good morning, Albert."

"That's easy for you to say."

Helen watches Einstein shift uncomfortably in the chair.

"Are you feeling alright?"

"I'm fine."

"You look like hell."

"I love you too."

Helen smiles. But the look of deep concern for Einstein's well-being never leaves her face.

"You've had another nightmare, haven't you?"

Einstein minimizes. "It's nothing."

Helen has a frustrated edge to her voice when she responds. "I don't understand you. Why do you keep putting yourself through this? Do you enjoy suffering that much?"

Einstein shrugs. "I've learned to live with it."

"Why live with it when Carl can help you?"

"How do you know he can help me? How do you know anybody can help me? No one ever has before."

"He's one of the most brilliant minds in the field. His specialty is dream analysis." She pauses. "Why am I telling you this? You know as well as I do he can help you."

"He's in Germany. He's old and frail like me."

"You <u>hate</u> asking people for help. You've got to do <u>everything</u> yourself, don't you?"

"That's not it."

"Why even bother denying it, Albert? I know you better than anybody. Including yourself."

A gentle smile creeps across Einstein's face. "Perhaps you do, Helen."

Helen drives home her point. "He's your friend. Nothing would make him happier than to be able to give you something in return for all that you've given him over the years. Don't be selfish, Albert. Don't deprive him of the opportunity to help you."

Einstein sighs deeply. "All right, Helen. Call him."

4

Two small figures in the distance walk across the snow-covered Princeton University campus on a bleak, overcast day. It is Christmas recess. The campus quad is devoid of all but a few students, lending an atmosphere of loneliness and isolation.

One of the figures is Carl Jung, in his eighties. His mind is alert. His eyes are alive with energy and a childlike wonder, in spite of his many years and the apparent frailness of his body. Einstein walks beside him, bundled up in an over-coat, a woolen cap pulled over his head.

"Things are not very bright, Carl. I feel as if I were flying in an airplane high up in the sky without knowing how, or even if, I will ever reach the ground."

"I know what you're going through, Albert. I've had periods of frustration in my work as well."

"This is more than a 'period,' Carl. I've been trying to discover a Unified Field Theory for thirty-six <u>years</u>. And I'm no closer today than I was when I first started. Do you have any idea what that's like?"

"No. I can't say that I do."

"You know what's really disturbing? The possibility that I stumbled across the answer in some primitive form, but didn't recognize it at the time. It's a little late for me to start reviewing thirty-six years' worth of ideas."

"Whether you did or didn't touch upon the answer in the past doesn't mat-ter, Albert. The answer you seek exists <u>now</u>. In the Collective Unconscious."

Einstein smiles gently at his old friend. "You'll never stop trying to turn me into a mystic, will you?"

"I'm not trying to convert you. I'm trying to help you to see the truth. It makes life a lot easier when you understand the rules of the game."

"What rules?"

"The moment you had the desire to discover a Unified Field Theory, it came into existence. The completed formula is in your mind right now. You're just having trouble getting to it. You refuse to accept what you've asked for and have already been given."

"I obviously don't know how to do that."

"Of course you do! You did it when you discovered that $E=mc^2$."

"Then why don't I do it now?"

"Resistance. You're subconsciously blocking yourself."

"Why?"

"From the description of your dream, I would say guilt over the atomic bomb. And perhaps fear that the discovery of a Unified Field Theory would yield a weapon of even greater destruction. I wouldn't be surprised if there were other unresolved issues in that thick skull of yours as well."

"I see. And what do you propose to do about it?"

"With hypnotic regression we will bring forgotten memories to consciousness so that we can discuss them and relieve your blockage."

5

Einstein lies on a couch in his study. He's in an hypnotic trance. Jung sits beside him in a chair, conducting the hypnotic regression session.

"Where are you, Albert?"

"In a lecture hall at the University of Berlin."

"What year is it?"

**

A huge banner across the front wall reads: "1919 Symposium on Quantum Mechanics." Another sign reads: "Guest Speaker: Wolfgang Pauli."

Pauli, in his twenties, stands at the front of the lecture hall. He is a vibrant, passionate speaker who infects people with his enthusiasm and energy, transforming a straight-forward, scientific lecture into performance art.

As he addresses his audience, he refers to two drawings on the blackboard: (1) A box with a cat standing up inside it, and (2) A box with a cat lying dead inside it.

"… And so the cat in the box is neither alive nor dead but in an <u>in between</u> state," lectures Pauli. "Once we look inside the box, we have then, and <u>only then</u>, defined reality. Then, and <u>only then</u>, is the cat either alive or dead." He pauses. "What determines whether the cat is alive or dead? The movement of an electron from one energy level to another. Movement which doesn't occur for <u>any particular reason</u>. It just <u>happens</u>!... <u>Spontaneously</u>... <u>Randomly</u>!..."

Someone shouts out from the back of the room. "<u>Preposterously</u>!"

All heads turn to see who has challenged Professor Pauli. Mouths drop open in awe when they spot young Albert Einstein standing in the back of the room.

"Tell me something, Professor Pauli. Can your precious Quantum Theory stand up to a little critical analysis?," asks Einstein.

Pauli grins. "You have the floor, Professor."

Einstein walks to the front of the room, all eyes riveted on him.

"First of all, the cat <u>cannot</u> be in some 'indeterminate' state. Whether or not we open the box and look inside, <u>something has happened</u>! Furthermore, future research will one day determine <u>why</u> an electron transition occurs when it does. <u>Proving</u> that randomness and spontaneity have <u>nothing</u> to do with it."

"Professor Einstein..."

"Call me Albert."

"Very well. You're wrong, Albert."

"Why can't <u>you</u> face the fact that Quantum Mechanics is incomplete? How can you be so blind to the obvious?"

"I was just going to ask you the same thing," Pauli retorts.

"Oh really? Wasn't Sir Isaac Newton's Theory believed to be the absolute truth of things for more than two hundred years? And did I not prove his theory to be incomplete?"

"No matter how incomplete Quantum Mechanics might or might not be, uncertainty and chance at the subatomic, quantum level is indisputable!"

"No! There <u>must</u> be some underlying clockwork that keeps the universe running and only gives the <u>appearance</u> of uncertainty and unpredictability at the sub-atomic level. God does <u>not</u> play dice with the universe!"

"He does indeed play dice! God has his gaming tables in <u>every</u> atom and <u>every</u> cubic millimeter of empty space! This is <u>fact</u>!"

Einstein is unshaken. "No. Today's 'fact' will be tomorrow's fiction."

"We shall see."

"Indeed we shall."

**

Einstein and Pauli walk across the now-empty lecture hall toward the exit. Pauli remarks to Einstein.

"With the exception of our debate, that was one of the most boring confer-ences I have ever attended."

Einstein nods in agreement. "While I was listening to those horrid speakers I came up with a new definition of eternity."

Pauli laughs. "How about joining me in a drink?"

"Why not?"

"Excellent. There's a good friend of mine I want you to meet. His name is Carl Jung."

6

Carl Jung, in his mid-forties, is drinking with Einstein and Pauli in a small pub. At the moment he is explaining one of his pet theories.

"I believe that the universe is an energy matrix in which <u>everything</u> is connected. Consequently, when events occur which appear, on the surface, to be coincidental and meaningless, there is actually a meaningful connection underlying them, even if we can't see the meaning. That connection I call synchronicity."

Einstein is skeptical. "You're speaking of a <u>non</u>-causal connecting principle."

"Yes."

"That I cannot accept. I favor a <u>causally</u>-dominated universe in which <u>nothing</u> takes place that does not have an ultimate cause. What you postulate is a romanticized view of reality. Such is the stuff of mysticism, not science."

"One day you may discover that you're a mystic, too."

Einstein chuckles. "I seriously doubt that."

With that, Pauli raises his wine glass in the air. "I'd like to propose a toast."

Einstein and Jung pick up their glasses and raise them in the air as well.

"To Truth!," Pauli proclaims. "<u>Whatever</u> it one day reveals itself to be!"

The three men clink their wine glasses and exclaim in unison, "To Truth!"

**

Einstein, Pauli, and Jung stumble drunkenly down the street together, giggling and mumbling amongst themselves. When Einstein loses his balance and falls against some garbage cans, making a racket, a woman pokes her head out a nearby window and yells at Einstein.

"Get off the street, you worthless drunk!"

Pauli reacts, shouts back at her, his words slurred. "Thish is no worshlesh drunk, madam. Thish drunk is Albert Einshtein!"

"And I'm Kaiser Wilhelm! Go home, you crazy, drunken fools!"

Einstein bursts into laughter. It's a big, warm infectious belly laugh that ignites Jung and Pauli's laughter as well.

7

It's a few nights later. Einstein, Pauli, and Jung are drinking wine in Einstein's study, his inner sanctum. A portrait painting of Sir Isaac Newton looks down on them from the wall. Einstein hands cigars out to his friends.

"It's <u>incredible</u> the number of requests I get to endorse various products. I've received letters from manufacturers of toilet waters, disinfectants, musical instruments, clothes. There was one company that wanted to come out with an 'Einstein Cigar.'"

Pauli shakes his head. "What foolishness."

"You mean 'What <u>shamelessness</u>,' don't you? It's pathetic. People selling their reputation to the highest bidder."

"A sad commentary on the commercialism and corruption of our times," Jung replies.

Einstein reaches for the wine bottle. Pours himself and the others more wine. As he raises his glass and takes a sip, some wine spills on his vest. He barely takes notice of it. Not so with Pauli, the obsessive-compulsive that he is.

"If you douse that with cold water a stain won't set."

Einstein shrugs, unmoved by such trivial concerns.

"For your wife's sake," Pauli adds.

"Elsa accepts me as I am. She doesn't mind cleaning up after me."

"I'm sure she loves every minute of it."

Pauli's pointed sarcasm hits its intended mark. Einstein has second thoughts. Decides to take off his jacket and do what Pauli has suggested. As he proceeds to remove his jacket, Pauli shouts at him.

"Wait!"

"What?!"

Pauli has a mischievous twinkle in his eye. "I've heard, Albert, that you can't resist an interesting challenge. Is that true?"

"What do you propose?," Einstein chuckles.

"I bet you can't take off your vest without removing your jacket."

Jung turns to Pauli and asks incredulously, "You want him to take off his vest while his jacket is on <u>over it</u>?"

"That's the deal."

Einstein laughs. "It appears that the rumors about you are true, Wolfgang. You <u>are</u> a wild man."

Pauli grins. "Thank you."

"My pleasure. Now then. What are the stakes?"

"Loser buys dinner for the three of us."

"I like this bet," Jung chimes in.

"I can see why you would." Einstein turns back to Pauli. "You're on."

Jung watches with a mixture of amusement and amazement as possibly the greatest mind of the century, if not of all time, begins a series of elaborate gyrations and contortions, trying to maneuver out of his vest with his jacket still on. As Einstein doesn't seem to be making any headway, Pauli clucks with delight.

"No way. No chance. No how."

Einstein is breathing heavily now. Beads of perspiration form on his brow as he continues to struggle with the vest.

"Give it up, old man," Pauli chuckles.

Einstein grunts, "No way... no chance... no how."

Einstein continues wrestling with the vest. Pauli starts getting nervous when it looks like Einstein might be making some progress.

After a few more contortions, Einstein makes a final tortuous twist, and... He's done it! He triumphantly waves his crumpled vest in the air. Pauli is astonished.

"I don't believe it!"

Einstein lets out his trademark belly laugh. Pauli turns to Jung. "I can't believe he did that! Can you believe he did that?! I can't believe he did that!"

Einstein's infectious laughter continues. Soon all three men are laughing uproariously.

8

The University of Berlin lecture hall is packed with people. A banner on the wall reads: "Society For Social Responsibility." Einstein is at the podium. He addresses the audience with great conviction, intensity and passion.

"Heroism on command. Senseless violence. All the loathsome nonsense that goes by the name of patriotism. How passionately I hate them! How vile and despicable war seems to me! I would rather be hacked in pieces than take part in such an abominable business!"

Einstein looks out at the crowd of listeners. They wait in breathless anticipation. When he begins speaking again, his voice is almost a whisper. Yet because everyone's attention is totally focused on him, each word is heard clearly and passionately.

"Never do anything against your conscience. Even if the State demands it. Conscience is what separates man from the beasts. Conscience is the difference between heaven and hell."

Einstein pauses. "One is forever confronted by the temptation to play it safe and to follow the pack. Don't yield to this temptation. Be willing to search for and discover the beat of your own internal drummer. Be ever vigilant, ever attentive to the true nature of your being. Thank you and good evening."

The audience responds with resounding applause.

9

A thunderstorm in progress. Einstein has a violin crooked in his neck. He's improvising a brooding, angst-ridden melody flooded with somber, mournful, longing tones. He is filled with frustration and discouragement. His music reflects this mood.

After a few moments, Einstein puts down the violin. He moves to his cluttered desk which is overflowing with crumpled notes and scribbled calculations. He grabs a piece of paper and jots down an idea.

He is so deep in thought, he doesn't hear his wife Elsa enter the room. She is in her late thirties, plain-looking, a little on the heavy side. It's obvious that she is devoted to her husband.

"Albert."

Einstein looks up at her.

"You're not going to stay up all night again, are you?"

Einstein responds with a burst of manic energy. "I <u>must</u>! I'm locked in a problem of <u>incalculable</u> proportions!"

"You're driving yourself to exhaustion, Albert. You've got to get some rest."

"You don't understand, Elsa. I've got a gaping hole in my Relativity Theory! If I don't make a breakthrough, I'll go crazy!"

"No. If you keep pushing yourself like this, you'll go crazy. Trust me. You're already starting to sound like a raving lunatic. <u>Please</u>, Albert. Come to bed."

"Even if I resolve the loophole in my Relativity Theory, I could <u>still</u> hit a dead end. It's entirely possible that physics cannot be based on the Unified Field concept. In which case, <u>nothing</u> will remain of my entire castle in the air, Relativity Theory included!"

Elsa strokes his forehead. "Albert. My dear, sweet Albert. Do you realize how long it's been since we've made love?"

Einstein sighs deeply. His face softens. He looks up into Elsa's caring, longing eyes. After a beat, he stands up. Takes Elsa's face in his hands and kisses her gently on the lips.

"It has been a long time, hasn't it?"

She nods and smiles as he leads her to the door. Just before getting there, Einstein abruptly stops in his tracks, as if hit by a bolt of lightning.

"<u>That's it</u>!"

"What? What's it?"

"A device which generates an electro-magnetic field! If I could synchronize the frequency of that field with my electrical brainwave activity…"

"Albert."

"… I <u>might</u> be able to super-fire my neurons, boost my brain-power, and overcome my mental block!"

"Albert."

Einstein rushes back to his desk. Starts jotting down some of his thoughts.

"This is <u>definitely</u> a project for the Habicht Brothers. They'll know exactly what to do!"

"Albert!"

"Just a few more minutes, Elsa."

"It's <u>always</u> 'just a few more minutes.'"

"Please try to understand, Elsa. I could spend the rest of my life searching for the Unified Field Theory and <u>never find it</u>! Do you realize how pathetic that would be?!"

"You could spend the rest of your life searching for the Unified Field Theory, never find it, <u>and</u> end up having wasted precious moments that we could have shared together. Do you realize how pathetic <u>that</u> would be?!"

**

76-Year-Old Einstein opens his eyes as he comes out of hypnosis and finds himself in his Princeton study with Carl Jung beside him. He looks at Jung for a moment, his face a mask of remorse.

"Elsa was right. I wasted the time we had together chasing a pipe dream." He sighs deeply. "You know, in a way, she was lucky that she died so young. Spared herself decades of pain and frustration she would have had to endure living with me."

Tears well up in his eyes. "I never told her how much I loved her."

Jung puts a consoling arm on Einstein's shoulder, but it does little to assuage his sadness.

10

Einstein is seated at his desk in his Physics Department study at Princeton University. Chancellor Smith, a tall, distinguished-looking man in his late 50s, with graying temples and dark, penetrating eyes, sits across from him. There is a palpable tension between these two men. Einstein addresses Smith.

"I don't appreciate your constant surveillance of my work."

"As head of the Physics Department it's my job to inquire about the progress of my research staff. And regardless of your antipathy for authority figures, may I remind you that it is your responsibility to comply with my request for information."

"Fine.," Einstein replies curtly. "Allow me to give you my report: I have no new information. Happy now?"

"I don't understand your hostility, Albert. You act like I'm your adversary. I'm not. I'm on your side. I've always been supportive of the work you do."

"Yes, but not for the sake of the work itself. Not for the purity of the truth I'm seeking."

"You're way off-base, Albert."

"I don't think so. I think the minute I finalize my Unified Field Theory, you're going to be on the phone with your Pentagon pals in Washington, figuring out some way to turn my work into new weapons of destruction."

"That's simply not true. You have no basis whatsoever for believing that."

"I have my intuition."

"You're a scientist. Stick to facts, not whimsy!"

"Had I stuck to the facts and ignored my intuition, I never would have dis-covered my Relativity Theory. So don't presume to tell me that my intuition is whimsical!"

"Look, Albert..."

Just then, Helen enters the office with a box in her hands. "Oh, excuse me, I didn't realize..."

"It's all right, Helen. Chancellor Smith was just leaving."

Chancellor Smith gets up, nods goodbye, and exits the office.

"What was that all about?," Helen inquires of Einstein.

"The usual." Einstein refers to the box Helen's holding. "What have you got there?"

"The box you asked for from the trunk in the attic."

"Excellent."

Helen places the box on the desk before Einstein. He stares at it with the eager anticipation of a child about to open a Christmas present. As he pulls back the flaps of the box, his eyes twinkle with the delight of warm recognition:

"My little machine!"

Einstein pulls out of the box a very primitive and bulky helmet which has scorched and tangled wires protruding from the top of it. Einstein is transfixed.

"What is that, Albert?," asks Helen.

"An invention I worked on with the Habicht Brothers in Berlin."

"Why have you kept it a secret all these years?"

Einstein shrugs his shoulders. "I was an emotional wreck. Full of anxiety and frustration. On the verge of physical exhaustion. Making no progress whatso-ever. I feared that a loophole existed which would eventually prove my Relativity Theories false. From all that," he says, referring to the helmet, "came this. A desperate effort to stimulate my mind."

"And did it?"

"No. It shorted-out the few times I tried using it. And I nearly electrocuted myself in the process. Fortunately, a short time later I broke through my block and came up with the idea for the Cosmological Constant. I never had the desire to try it again after that." Einstein pauses for a moment. "Until now."

"You're not seriously considering using that thing again, are you?"

Einstein ignores her question. "That grad student who came by a few weeks ago. The electrical engineer?"

"Robertson."

"Yes. Please call him for me. He might be able to help."

"Help what? Help you to kill yourself?!"

"Helen…"

"Don't 'Helen' me. You said the damn thing nearly electrocuted you the last time you tried it. I won't be a part of this, Albert!"

"Be realistic, Helen. What have I got to lose? My aneurysm could burst any day now. We both know I'm living on borrowed time as it is."

"Oh, so that means you should help it along?! That means you should risk your life on some foolhardy invention that probably won't do anything even if it doesn't explode in your face?!"

Einstein sighs deeply. He gets up from his desk, walks to the window, and looks outside. Some students are building a snowman on the quad. He stares at them for a few moments.

And then Einstein responds to Helen, but it's as if he's talking more to himself than to her. "The years of anxious searching in the dark. With their intense longing. Their alternations of confidence and exhaustion. And the final glorious emergence into light. Only those who have experienced it can understand it."

"I wish you wouldn't, Albert," pleads Helen.

Einstein continues to stare out the window. He appears deep in thought. In reality, he's recalling a similar situation that occurred many years ago.

**

40-Year-Old Einstein stares out the window of his Berlin apartment. Behind him his brand-new "little machine" sits on the table. Also behind him is his wife Elsa, a deeply worried look on her face.

"I wish you wouldn't, Albert," pleads Elsa.

**

76-Year-Old Einstein continues to stare out the window. His eyes get watery. A teardrop rolls down his cheek. He sighs deeply. And then walks back to his desk. Finally, he addresses Helen, who shares the same deeply worried look on her face that Elsa had on hers some forty years earlier.

"Very well, Helen. You needn't call Robertson." Einstein places his burnt-out little machine back in the box. Helen, deeply relieved, goes over to Einstein, puts her arms around him, and hugs him as if for dear life. She whispers in his ear, "Thank you, Albert. Thank you."

11

Einstein is in the Princeton University Science Auditorium addressing a roomful of students, who are listening with rapt attention.

"I still work incessantly on my scientific pursuits. And I am more certain than ever that Quantum Mechanics is incomplete. I maintain that the Unified Field Theory will not only incorporate all the forces of nature into <u>one unified law</u>, but will also provide the basis for a <u>new interpretation</u> of Quantum Mechanics."

Einstein pauses for a moment and surveys his audience. "As you embark on new careers as scientists and scholars, I want to leave you with these thoughts – No matter what your beliefs may be. No matter who or how many people agree or disagree with you… <u>Never stop questioning</u>. Curiosity has its own reason for existence. And its own reward. Never lose a holy curiosity. Thank you and good luck."

The audience jumps to its feet en masse, and explodes into a frenzy of cheers and applause. The standing ovation continues as Helen slowly escorts Einstein away from the podium and down the aisle. As they pass two young colleagues, they overhear one whispering to the other.

"Will you look at this?! The old man hasn't done a damn thing in over thirty years, and the people are <u>still</u> going nuts!"

His colleague nods in agreement. "The guy's a dinosaur! He's a joke! He'll <u>never</u> discover anything new!"

"Why can't he just retire gracefully and go away already?!"

Einstein winces, stung by the cruel remarks. Helen notices Einstein's reaction, leans into him.

"Don't listen to them, Albert. What do they know?"

Einstein looks at her. "The truth maybe?"

12

Einstein is tossing and turning in his sleep. He's dreaming. "Nightmaring" would be more accurate: Einstein is at the bottom of the ocean, frantically swimming upward toward the light at the surface. But no matter how hard and fast he swims, he fails to get any closer to the top.

**

Einstein sits on the porch in a rocking chair, staring up at the full moon, lost in his thoughts. Helen sits in a rocking chair beside him with an appointment book in her lap.

"On Friday afternoon you've got the faculty luncheon. On Saturday night you'll be giving the keynote speech at the Conference on Theoretical Physics. And on Sunday I thought we'd go to the lake. How's that sound?"

Einstein is quiet for a moment. Then he turns to Helen. "I don't <u>care</u> what Quantum Mechanics says! I <u>refuse</u> to believe that reality is based on random, spontaneous, chance events! There is order to the universe. There is precision! There is predictability. Based on natural, unalterable physical <u>laws</u>!"

Helen's heard a version of this rant hundreds of times before. And her answer is always reassuringly the same.

"You'll figure it out, Albert. I know you will. I have faith in you."

Einstein shakes his head. "I wish I had your faith. I don't anymore." He pauses a moment. "I've changed my mind, Helen. I'm going to re-design my machine and give it another try."

"Why, Albert? Because of what your colleagues said?"

"Do you think I want to die knowing the last 36 years of my life were a total waste?! I'd like to get to the truth. <u>Whatever</u> it is. Be right or be wrong so others can go forward and make some progress."

"Albert…"

"I've <u>got</u> to try <u>anything</u> I can! <u>Anything</u>! I've <u>got</u> to!!"

Helen is upset, but never having seen Einstein this frustrated before, she yields her position with grace and understanding.

"I'll call Jim Robertson in the morning."

Einstein turns his head to stare up at the moon once again. His gaze is transfixed, an eternal longing reflected in his eyes.

13

Einstein is working in the garden, pruning a rose bush. Wolfgang Pauli, now in his late fifties, assists him. Pauli looks older than he is, ravaged by years of stressful living and heavy drinking. He's nervous and jittery, unable to sit still.

Einstein opens the conversation. "So tell me, Wolfgang, what are you working on these days? I haven't heard from you in over a month!"

"I'm grappling with the Fine-Structure Constant."

Einstein is shocked. "You're actually spending time trying to figure out why Alpha equals 137?!"

Pauli nods yes. Einstein shakes his head in disbelief.

"Wolfgang. A dozen physicists including Heisenberg spent <u>years</u> at it and failed. Came up with nothing."

Pauli shrugs. "That was them. I'm me. Besides, I'm convinced that the mystery of Alpha is somehow tied into Quantum Mechanics."

"Dubious."

"What can I tell you? I've got this feeling… like it's something I'm supposed to do."

Einstein scrutinizes Pauli. He can't help but wonder if Pauli is perhaps a bit unstable.

"It nearly drove Heisenberg crazy. You know that, don't you?"

Pauli grins. "Then I've got nothing to worry about. I'm <u>already</u> crazy!"

Einstein laughs. Shakes his head. "You should get married again. It would be good for you."

"Why?," replies Pauli. "You never did."

"My wife died. Yours divorced you. There's a difference. Besides, I have Helen."

"And I have my wine bottle. So we both have a constant companion."

Einstein laughs again. Just then, Helen steps into the backyard. Einstein looks up at her.

"Jim Robertson is here."

14

Jim Robertson, a man in his late twenties, sits at the dinner table with Einstein, Pauli, and Helen. He has several scientific journal abstracts strewn across the table in front of him. He's giving an overview of them to the others.

"That covers the existing research on neural devices relating to brain augmentation and expanded consciousness. I recommend you make modifications on your device consistent with this research."

"Very well," replies Einstein. "The question now remains who has the technological aptitude for a task of this nature."

Robertson seems hesitant. Torn with conflict. Einstein picks up on it. "What is it, James? What's wrong?"

"There are risks, Professor. If anything were to happen to you..."

"Please. I am an old corpse with a lifetime of questions. I absolve you of any responsibility."

Robertson pauses a moment. "There is someone."

**

Professor Gould's electrical engineering laboratory contains high-tech equipment, miscellaneous devices and electrical apparatus. The walls of the lab are covered with surrealistic and psychedelic artwork of Dali, Magritte, Bosch, and others.

A bookshelf contains medical and scientific books, as well as religious, spiritual and mystical books, including The New Testament, The Baghavad Gita, The Koran, The Doors Of Perception, and The History of Psychedelics.

Professor Gould, in his thirties, has a tape measure wrapped around Einstein's head and is measuring the distance from one point on Einstein's skull to another. Pauli and Robertson stand beside them.

Gould philosophizes as he takes Einstein's measurements. "I believe that every past event that has happened exists now, but in a separate dimension. And every future event yet to happen exists now, but in a separate dimension. And just as one radio station is not audible to listeners tuned to another, so are these other realities not perceptible to us. At least, not under normal circumstances."

Pauli nods enthusiastically. "I'll take it one step further! Every past event that could have happened but didn't, and every future event that yet could happen but won't, also exists now, in separate dimensions."

"Keep talking like that and Carl will have you on medication in no time," Einstein interjects.

"Maybe you're the one who's crazy for thinking reality doesn't work this way!"

"Oh really? What you suggest contradicts every premise we hold dear about the way the physical universe operates."

"Picky, picky, picky."

Einstein laughs, then addresses Professor Gould. "How long do you think it will take you to make the modifications on my machine?"

"A week, maybe two, at the most."

15

Einstein talks to Robertson as they walk down the street toward Einstein's house.

"Human beings have become slaves of bathrooms, cars, radios, and millions of other technological goodies, which I believe will ultimately rob us of our spirit and individuality. Consequently, I resist the temptation of technology as much as I possibly can."

Einstein points to his hair. "Long hair minimizes the need for the barber." He points to his feet. "Socks can be done without." He points to the leather jacket he's wearing. "One leather jacket solves the coat problems for many years. Suspenders are superfluous, as are nightshirts and pajamas."

"I see what you're saying, Professor," responds Robertson. "But aren't the fruits of technology part of what progress and growth are all about? Making life more comfortable? Is that so bad?"

"It's a double-edged sword, my young friend. Both a blessing and a curse."

Einstein and Robertson approach Einstein's house. Einstein continues his discourse.

"The objects of human efforts – possessions, outward success, luxuries – have always seemed contemptible to me. I am convinced that no wealth in the world can help move humanity forward, even in the hands of the most devoted worker. Can you imagine Moses, Jesus, or Gandhi armed with the moneybags of Carnegie? No. Money only appeals to selfishness, and irresistibly invites abuse.

The <u>example</u> of great and pure individuals is the <u>only</u> thing that can lead us to noble thoughts and deeds."

They continue walking for a few moments. Robertson breaks the silence with a question.

"Do you believe in God, Professor?"

"I believe in Spinoza's God, who reveals himself in the orderly harmony of what exists. Not in a God who concerns himself with fates and actions of human beings."

"An impersonal God?"

"Yes. An impersonal God. A deterministic universe. A churchless religion. Disregard of money and material gains. World government. Pacifism and social-ism. All of these are generally thought to be un-American and, more or less, subversive. I believe in them all."

Einstein chuckles at this as they arrive in front of his house. But the wry, amused expression on his face quickly evaporates when he bends down to pick up the evening newspaper and sees the headline: "RED SCARE CONTINUES! McCARTHY HEARINGS IN THIRD WEEK!"

Einstein shakes his head sadly. "A Nazi propagandist once said, 'The great masses of people will more easily fall victim to a great lie than to a small one.' And so history repeats itself. And the majority of fools remain invincible."

Einstein sighs deeply. "It is easier to denature plutonium than to denature the evil spirit of man."

16

Chancellor Smith is sitting at Einstein's desk, going through Einstein's drawers, pulling out research notebooks. He starts leafing through one of the notebooks and examines its contents when Einstein opens the door and catches him in the act.

Chancellor Smith sputters, "Albert! I... uh... I..."

Einstein is furious. "What in blazes do you think you're doing?!"

"I... uh... was waiting for you, Albert. I... uh..."

"How <u>dare</u> you invade my privacy! How <u>dare</u> you look at my private journals!"

Chancellor Smith shifts to an offensive stance. "You're working for the Princeton University Physics Department. I am the head of that department. In other words, you're working for me. Or have you forgotten?"

"How <u>could</u> I forget?! You're always hovering over me!"

"That's my job, Albert. To keep the home fires burning."

"Is it also your job to snoop on me?"

"Sooner or later you're going to deliver these notes to my office. What's the harm in my..."

"You look at the notes when I give them to you! Not a moment sooner. Those were the terms of my work agreement. You've violated that agreement. I don't appreciate it."

"Forgive me, Albert. My curiosity got the better of me. I meant no disrespect. I didn't think…"

"Don't insult my intelligence. Your curiosity has nothing to do with it. Your friends in Washington are pressuring you for the status of my research."

"How many times do I have to tell you that's not true?," Chancellor Smith protests.

"I'm supposed to trust what you say? I'm supposed to believe somebody who sneaks into my office? You're no better than a common thief."

"I'm sorry you feel that way."

"So am I."

17

Einstein is in the bathroom, at the sink, his face lathered with shaving cream. He picks up a straight razor and draws the blade across his throat, severing his carotid artery and jugular vein. Blood spurts and gushes from his neck wounds.

**

Einstein bolts awake from his nightmare. His hand reflexively moves to his neck as he realizes it was just a dream.

**

Einstein is lying on the sofa. Jung sits in a chair beside him, dangling a pocketwatch on a chain in front of Einstein's face. His voice is soft and hypnotic.

"...As you continue to stare at the watch, you find yourself getting very, very sleepy. Your eyelids are feeling increasingly heavy. You are unable to keep them open..."

As Einstein stares at the watch his eyelids start to flutter. And then they close...

**

It's 1919 again. 40-Year-Old Einstein slowly walks down the stairs in his Berlin apartment toward the hallway leading to the kitchen. He stops to listen when he hears Elsa talking to Ingrid, a neighbor.

"I enjoy sharing the many honors which are bestowed on him," says Elsa. "But I miss the sympathy, the tenderness, the thoughtfulness which I crave. I find myself very alone in many respects. Very lonely."

Einstein reacts to Elsa's pain. Guilt and sadness wash across his face.

"Isn't it ironic," Ingrid responds, "that in spite of his love of humanity, he is totally detached from his environment and the human beings in it?"

Einstein winces.

Elsa responds to Ingrid's observation. "One might think that a genius such as he should be irreproachable in every respect. But no. Nature doesn't behave like that. Where she gives extravagantly, she takes away extravagantly."

"Come on, Elsa! He takes advantage of you. Treats you like a slave."

"You can't put him under one heading or another. You've got to see him all in one piece. God has given him so much nobility. Although life with him is exhausting and complicated and difficult at times, I find him wonderful. I really do."

"You're way too forgiving. Way too understanding."

"There's no such thing."

"What happened to the loneliness you were just telling me about? Can you honestly say it doesn't matter?"

Elsa sighs deeply. "No."

"You could teach him to treat you better. Men are trainable, you know."

"Not Albert. He rebels against all attempts at manipulation and control."

"He wouldn't change for you?"

"It's not in his nature."

"You call that love?"

Elsa is quiet for a moment. "I think he loves me."

"But you're not really sure, are you?"

Einstein feels terribly sad and terribly guilty. He starts down the steps again, this time loud enough for them to hear him in the kitchen and know he's approaching.

Einstein enters as Elsa finishes setting the table, He addresses her. "Good morning."

Elsa smiles warmly at him. "Sit, Albert. Breakfast will be ready in a few minutes."

Einstein takes a seat at the table across from Ingrid, who stares at him with a severe, disdainful expression. He shifts uncomfortably in his seat as Elsa places a glass of juice and a cup of tea in front of him. Elsa moves to the stove and begins scrambling some eggs as Ingrid confronts Einstein.

"I don't understand something, Albert. Maybe you can help me."

"I'll be glad to try."

"Elsa does everything for you. I'm wondering: What do you do for her?"

Elsa gasps. "Ingrid!"

"What? I just asked a question." She turns back to Einstein. "Well?"

"I give her my love."

"Do you?"

"Ingrid!," Elsa interjects.

Ingrid gets up. "I'll talk to you later, Elsa."

Ingrid exits. Elsa, embarrassed by Ingrid's brazen confrontation with Einstein, turns back to the stove and continues scrambling the eggs.

Einstein looks at her for several beats. He yearns to say something loving and reassuring to her, but can't find the words.

Einstein sighs deeply. He gets up from the table, walks over to Elsa, and stands behind her. Still unable to articulate his feelings, he watches as she stirs the eggs in the frying pan. He becomes transfixed, hypnotized by the swirling motion Elsa is making with the eggs. Clockwise, then counterclockwise, then clockwise again, then counter-clockwise again.

Einstein is suddenly struck by an inspirational thought triggered by the swirling motions. He rushes back to the table, sits down, and snatches a pencil from his shirt pocket.

As Elsa brings the frying pan over to the table to scoop some eggs onto Einstein's plate, she sees him scribbling equations on the tablecloth.

"That's a new tablecloth, Albert!"

"Huh? Oh… I, uh…" Einstein sighs. "Forgive me, Elsa. I just don't think sometimes."

"Do you know how funny that sounds coming from you, a genius, who is world-famous for what he thinks?"

"I know… I'm sorry."

Elsa has a gentle, forgiving smile on her face. "You'd better eat your eggs before they get cold."

Einstein nods. He picks up his fork and starts eating.

"Don't forget to come home early today, Albert. We've got that faculty dinner this evening."

"You'd better cancel it. Tell them I'm sick or something."

"You can't do that!," Elsa bristles. "It's in your honor! People are counting on you being there!"

"I can't afford the time, Elsa. I've got too much work to do."

Elsa explodes. "You've <u>always</u> got too much work to do! What are you going to do? Spend every minute in your mind, inside yourself, closed off from the rest of the world?!"

Einstein says nothing in response. Elsa stares at him for a few moments, then entreats him.

"Please, Albert! Do this one thing for me?! Give me one night when you're not totally consumed with your work! Is that too much to ask?!"

18

A banner on the Berlin banquet hall wall reads: "ANNUAL FACULTY CLUB AWARDS DINNER." Dozens of tables filled with people are peppered throughout the room.

Standing at a podium at the front of the room is Wolfgang Pauli, reciting a poem he has concocted in honor of Albert Einstein. It's a parody of "The Walrus and the Carpenter."

"You hold that time is badly warped, that even light is bent. I think I get the idea there, if this is what you meant: The mail the postman brings today, tomorrow will be sent."

The audience laughs, amused and delighted by Pauli's poem.

At Einstein's table, Elsa is seated beside Einstein, who is furiously scribbling equations on the back of the dinner program, oblivious to everything going on around him.

Pauli recites the poem's last verse: "The shortest line, Einstein replied, is not the one that's straight. It curves around upon itself, much like a figure eight. And if you go too rapidly you will arrive too late."

The audience laughs and applauds. Pauli bows. When the applause dies down, Pauli speaks.

"Thank you very much, ladies and gentlemen. And now it's my pleasure to introduce the greatest intellect on the planet – my esteemed colleague and my dearest friend – Albert Einstein!"

The audience rises to its feet, turns toward Einstein's table, and gives him a rousing and passionate standing ovation! Einstein, totally self-absorbed as usual, is oblivious to the thunderous clapping all around him.

Elsa leans over to him and whispers in his ear, "You have to get up, Albert."

Einstein does as he is told. Rises to his feet. Starts clapping his hands along with the others.

"No, Albert," Elsa whispers. "They're clapping for you!"

Embarrassed, Einstein sheepishly stops clapping, composes himself, then leans into Elsa and whispers, "Now I go on the trapeze."

Einstein heads toward the podium. Upon arriving there, he shakes Pauli's hand. Then he removes a sheet of paper from his coat pocket, unfolds it, clears his throat, and begins his speech.

"The murder of men is disgusting to me. My pacifism is based on my deepest antipathy to every kind of cruelty and hatred. Time and time again, people ask me, 'Is there any way of delivering mankind from the menace of war?' To this I have always said: One does not make wars less likely to occur by formulating rules of warfare."

Einstein pauses briefly, then continues. "War cannot be humanized. It can only be abolished. How? People must refuse all military service. People must refuse to lend support of any kind."

Einstein pauses again. Looks out at his audience and then continues his speech with deep conviction. "If another war broke out I would unconditionally refuse to do war service, direct or indirect, and would try to persuade my friends to take the same stand, regardless of how the cause of the war should be judged."

19

76-Year-Old Einstein is still under hypnosis. Jung comments on the previous hypnotic regression.

"And yet some twenty years later, as World War II loomed on the horizon, you were persuading your friends to do the exact opposite."

Einstein responds with a voice full of sadness.

"Yes. This is true."

"I want you to go forward along your life-line, Albert," Jung suggests. "Forward in years to that particular time when you reversed your pacifist position."

**

The year is 1938. The place is Washington, D.C.. The White House. A garden party is in progress. The front lawn is filled with politicians and celebrities. A banner proclaims: "Welcome to America, Albert Einstein!"

Einstein is holding a conversation with President Franklin Delano Roosevelt. There is passion and conviction in Einstein's voice.

"Hitler has to be stopped! Were I a Belgian, I would <u>not</u> refuse military service."

Roosevelt reflects on this for a moment and then responds. "Isn't that a little strange coming from the same man who said, 'I would rather be hacked in pieces than take part in such an abominable business as war'?"

"Yes, it is a little strange. It proves, once again, that everything is relative. Even in pacifism there are no absolutes." Einstein pauses a moment. "As paradoxical as it may seem, I am <u>still</u> a <u>convinced pacifist</u>! There are, however, circumstances in which I now believe the use of force and the sacrifice of human lives are appropriate – namely in the face of an enemy unconditionally bent on subverting and destroying mankind. As H. G. Wells said during World War I, 'Every sword that is drawn against Germany is now a sword of peace.'"

**

76-Year-Old Einstein comes out of hypnosis and ruefully contemplates his conflicting positions.

20

Einstein and Jung are seated in garden chairs. As the two men talk, Einstein's 8-Year-Old granddaughter, Elsa, stands on a wooden milk crate behind Einstein's chair, and is combing Einstein's hair.

"As to this issue of utilizing force as a means to an end," Einstein begins, "I have returned to my instinctive pacifism, looking on my need to oppose Hitler as 'the exception which proves the rule.' I still believe we should strive to do things in the spirit of Mohatma Gandhi: not to use violence in fighting for our cause, but rather non-participation in what we believe is evil."

"Gandhi would never have reversed his absolute position of non-violence as you did," Jung points out. "He would have said, 'Love has no exceptions. No opposites.'"

"Yes. You're quite right, Carl." Einstein sighs deeply. "That's what Gandhi meant when he talked of the power of love and forgiveness... that one must have <u>absolute</u> faith that they will work as a means to peace. Deep down I was lacking in that faith."

Einstein looks deeply saddened. "I did the best I could." Another deep sigh from Einstein. "I have made many errors of judgment in my life. It was a grave mistake when I signed the letter to President Roosevelt recommending that atom bombs be made."

"To be fair, Albert, there was some justification – the danger that Hitler would make them first."

EINSTEIN'S COSMIC JOURNEY

"And now I'm working on a theory which, theoretically, could lead to weapons capable of even far greater destruction. Where is the justification in that?"

Jung plays devil's advocate. "Should one stop seeking truth because evil men exist in the world?"

"I don't know, Carl. Maybe so."

Helen sticks her head out the back door. "Excuse me, Albert. It's time for lunch."

Einstein nods to Jung. "Shall we?"

Elsa, who has been combing Einstein's hair throughout their conversation, tries to remove the comb, only to discover that it's stuck! When she tugs at the comb with frustration, Einstein lets out a yelp.

"Sorry, Grampa."

Einstein brings his hand to his head and feels the tangled mess his granddaughter has left him with. He laughs heartily.

21

Albert's son, Hans Albert Einstein, 50, is seated at the dining table along with his daughter Elsa, Einstein, Helen, and Jung. They are in the midst of having lunch.

Hans Albert turns to his father. "I understand you're going to experiment with your invention again."

Einstein gives Helen a look, then turns back to Hans Albert. "Yes. I'm hoping it will stimulate my mind so that new inspirational thoughts and insights will occur to me."

"Thus enabling you to grasp the missing links in your Unified Field Theory?," Hans Albert asks.

Einstein nods. "And <u>finally</u> end the mystery that's been plaguing my existence for 36 years."

"What about the danger to your health?"

"Why are you asking me about things Helen has already told you?," Einstein asks with an annoyed edge to his voice.

"Is she right? Is there a risk here?"

"Of course there is. Anytime you experiment with something new and unknown, there's going to be a risk. But the risk is minimal compared to the potential knowledge I might gain. Besides, I've already got one foot in the grave as it is."

"I don't suppose you'd consider letting me test the machine for you, just to make sure it's safe?"

"No, son. I'm afraid not. I wouldn't feel right placing your life in jeopardy."

Helen interjects. "But placing <u>your</u> life in jeopardy is okay?!"

"I've lived a full life. I have no complaints."

"When exactly are you planning on doing this?"

"In three or four days."

"I wish I could be here, but I have to leave tomorrow. I've got a week's worth of meetings waiting for me."

"I understand, Hans. I appreciate you taking the time to visit. It's always good to see you and Elsa."

Eintstein observes Hans' look of concern.

"You needn't worry. I'm sure everything will go smoothly."

From the expressions on everyone's faces, Einstein has failed in his effort to reassure them.

22

Einstein's "little machine" sits on his desk in his study. It's been completely remodeled into a piece of high-tech, state-of-the-art hardware. Einstein straps the headpiece onto his head and flips the "on" switch. The headpiece starts humming.

After a few moments, smoke and sparks start shooting out of the top of the headpiece. Einstein's body starts convulsing. He's electrocuting himself!

**

Helen stands over the stove in the kitchen when she suddenly hears a loud thump coming from the room above her. Overcome with fear and dread, she drops her cooking utensils and races out of the room.

Helen enters Einstein's study, sees Einstein's motionless body lying on the floor. She gasps in horror, runs over to him, pulls the sparking and smoking headpiece off his head. As she kneels over him, her eyes well up with tears.

"Dear God, please don't take him from me! Please! Let him live! Please let him live!!"

And then something fantastical happens. Something imperceptible to the human eye. Einstein's astral body, ghostlike in nature, separates from his physical body and rises up toward the ceiling.

And then it passes through the ceiling and through the roof of the house. And then it whisks up into the clouds, up into the atmosphere, out into space, through a galaxy of stars, toward a massive black hole.

Einstein's astral body enters the black hole and is enveloped in darkness, except for a very faint, shimmering light far away in the distance.

As Einstein's astral body approaches the light, it becomes brighter, and begins to coalesce into the astral body of a woman. It is Elsa, Einstein's wife, who has been dead for over twenty-five years. She's smiling benevolently, her arms spread open in welcome.

Einstein's astral body faces Elsa's astral body. Einstein looks at her with awe and amazement, shock and confusion.

"Elsa? Is it really you?"

"Yes, Albert."

Einstein, overwhelmed with emotion, bursts into tears. Elsa takes him in her arms and embraces him tightly as he continues to sob.

"My dear, sweet Elsa. I've missed you so much. So very, very much." Einstein pauses. "Can you ever forgive me?"

"There's nothing to forgive."

"Yes there is. I was so self-absorbed. Self-obsessed. Forgive me for not showing you how much I loved and valued you."

"I forgive you, Albert. And I absolve you of the guilt you've been bearing on my behalf."

Suddenly Helen's voice booms out of the darkness.

"<u>Albert</u>!… <u>Albert</u>!"

"Helen?," asks Einstein.

Einstein looks at Elsa for an explanation.

"You must go back, Albert."

"No, Elsa! I won't! I want to stay here with you!"

"You must go back."

"But there's so much we need to talk about. So much that still needs to be said."

Helen's voice calls to him once more. "Albert!… Albert!"

Albert shouts back in response. "I won't go back! I <u>won't</u>!"

"You must," Elsa tells him. "It's not your time yet."

"But, Elsa…"

Her voice is soft and soothing. "You must go back."

Elsa's calm tone, her benevolent smile, and the overall grace of her demeanor has a reassuring and calming effect on Einstein. He hesitates for a few moments more, then nods his acceptance to return to his physical body. And with that, Einstein's astral body whisks backwards. Back through the black hole, back through the galaxy of stars, back down to the planet Earth, back down through the atmosphere, back through Einstein's house, back through the ceiling of Einstein's study, back down to Einstein's motionless body, where Helen is kneeling beside it.

Einstein's astral body merges with his physical body. A moment passes. And then Einstein's eyes open. Helen lets out a shout of ecstatic joy.

23

Einstein and Jung are walking across the Princeton campus to the physics building. Jung listens with excitement as Einstein describes his out-of-body experience.

"… and there she was… my Elsa. As young and as pretty as she was on our wedding day. Smiling at me with a love that perfused every aspect of my being."

"What a <u>fantastic</u> experience, Albert! To know with certainty that you are not a body, that death is just another moment in your life-line, that you are an eternal spirit which transcends time and space! What a blessing!"

"You're making the assumption that my experience was real. It could just as easily be explained as an hallucinatory experience."

"Do you really believe that?"

"A scientist cannot allow his personal biases, desires, or expectations to interfere with his interpretation of the facts. Although it is very appealing to consider that I might be a spirit capable of separating from my body and transcending death, if it is an hallucination I experienced, a perceptual aberration, then I am serving no purpose to promote the fantasy as truth. To do so would be a grave mistake. No pun intended."

"But in your gut, in your heart of hearts, deep in your bones, didn't it <u>feel</u> real? And when you returned to your body, was it like waking up from just another night's sleep? Or was there something more, something else?"

"It did have a 'feel' to it unlike anything I've ever experienced. I'll grant you that. But that, in itself, is not validation that my spirit left my body and traveled through the cosmos to communicate with my dead wife."

"You're a stubborn old man, Albert."

Einstein chuckles. "Now <u>that</u> I'll agree with."

Einstein's smile suddenly turns into a scowl at what he sees in front of the physics building.

Chancellor Smith is shaking hands with a man wearing a government-issue blue suit, who then gets into a car parked by the curb. The car pulls away. Einstein's face reflects his disdain for Chancellor Smith.

As Einstein and Jung continue walking toward the physics building, an idea occurs to Einstein.

"If my out-of-body experience really happened and was not an hallucination, then that 'astral state' should be reproducible. Under other conditions, I should be able to separate my astral body from my physical body."

"That's correct," replies Jung. "In fact, there are exercises and deep-relaxation meditations which have been designed to induce out-of-body experiences."

"Interesting," Einstein reflects. "Is it possible to select a particular person or place you wish to visit during one of these journeys out of the body?"

Jung nods. "From what I understand, all you have to do is think of the person or place you wish to visit, and you are automatically transported there." Jung pauses. "Why do you ask?"

Einstein nods toward Chancellor Smith, who is now entering the physics building.

"I have a theory about Chancellor Smith."

24

Literature on astral projection is strewn across Einstein's desk in his study. Einstein is lying on the sofa. His eyes are closed. He looks deeply relaxed and serene. After a few moments, Einstein's astral body, ghostlike in nature, separates from his physical body, rises up to the ceiling, and then passes through the ceiling.

Einstein's astral body rises out of the roof of the house and starts whisking across the city at an incredible speed. Within seconds it has left the city and is whisking across the countryside.

It is almost pitch-black. Almost impossible to perceive anything. Einstein's astral body arrives at a dark, foreboding place. After a moment, another astral body appears. And then another. And another. And another. And another. And they keep on coming!

Within moments Einstein's astral body is surrounded by hundreds of astral spirits pressing against him. As the astral spirits start sobbing and moaning, expressing an intensity of anguish and torment that is unbearable, Einstein's astral self becomes more and more terrified.

Fearing that he will go insane, and unable to endure much more of this hellish nightmare, Einstein opens his mouth and lets loose his own gut-wrenching scream. "Carlllllll!"

Instantly, Einstein's astral body separates from the mass of screaming astral spirits, and whisks off into the darkness.

Einstein's astral body passes through the roof of Carl Jung's house into Jung's study. Once there, Einstein's astral body witnesses Jung, who sits at his desk writing in his journal. He's dressed in striped pajamas, burgundy robe and brown slippers. He is totally oblivious to Einstein's astral presence.

Jung puts down his pen for a second. Picks up a decanter of wine. Pours himself a glass. Takes a few sips.

Einstein's astral body takes all of this in. His previous expression of sheer terror has now been replaced by astonishment and awe. He watches Jung, who puts down the wine glass and resumes writing.

After a few moments, Einstein has the presence of mind to proceed with the initial purpose of his astral experiment. He whispers to himself, "Chancellor Smith."

Instantly, Einstein's astral body whisks back up through the ceiling.

Einstein's astral body passes through the roof of Chancellor Smith's house into the Chancellor's bedroom. Chancellor Smith is lying in bed, reading a book. Einstein's astral body stares at Chancellor Smith for a few moments, and then walks out of the bedroom and into the study.

Einstein's astral body walks over to the desk and scans the various objects on the desk top: A physics journal abstract. A newspaper. A stack of unopened mail. A U.S. Pentagon file folder marked: "Advanced Weapons Systems – Top Secret."

Einstein's astral body tries to open the file folder, but his astral hands pass right through it.

**

Einstein's astral body drops down from the ceiling of his study and merges with Einstein's physical body, which is lying immobile on the sofa. After a moment, Einstein's eyes open. His expression reflects grave concern over the discovery of the file folder at Chancellor Smith's house.

25

Einstein and Jung are driving down the road. Einstein is relating to Jung the details of his out-of-body experience.

"There were astral bodies everywhere. Surrounding me. Pressing against me. Suffocating me. I thought I was going to go insane."

"Amazing," remarks Jung. "That reminds me of something that I experienced many years ago."

"What?"

"For several days my house was crammed full of spirits. They were packed deep, right up to the door. And the air was so thick it was scarcely possible to breathe."

"That's what happened to me!," exclaims Einstein.

"Yes, but I wasn't in an out-of-body state. I was awake and alert at the time."

"Incredible!"

Jung nods his agreement. "My doctor thought I was having a nervous break-down. At first, I did too."

"And then?," asks Einstein.

"I eventually concluded that I had witnessed something that was there. I had tapped into a perceptual experience that was <u>always</u> available to me, but which I had previously screened out of my vision."

"Interesting. What do you think enabled you to have the experience at the time that you did?"

"My mental readiness. I believe that when you're ready for the truth, it al-ways comes to you. Assuming your subconscious doesn't block the flow." Jung pauses. "The fact that you had the out-of-body experience last night indicates to me your own mental readiness for new information, perceptions, and insights. It indicates that you're letting go of some of the fear which has been blocking your progress up to now. Tell me what happened next."

"In my terror I called out your name. And in an instant was whisked to your house, to your study. You were at your desk writing in your journal and sipping on some wine. You were wearing striped pajamas, a burgundy robe, and brown slippers."

"You were in my study, Albert," Jung responds with excitement. "You've described the circumstances precisely. You were there!"

Einstein nods. "Which means that what we call reality is but the tip of the iceberg."

"There is literally a lot more than meets the eye," Jung agrees.

Einstein chuckles, but his light-heartedness is quickly replaced by an extremely sober expression. Jung notices.

"What's wrong, Albert?"

"Part of me was hoping the out-of-body experience was an hallucinatory fantasy."

"Why?"

"After I saw you, I visited Chancellor Smith and saw something extremely disturbing."

The car carrying Einstein and Jung pulls up to the curb in front of Wolfgang Pauli's apartment house. As Einstein and Jung get out of the car and walk toward the front door, Jung asks Einstein, "Did you read the file?"

"No. But that doesn't matter. The mere presence of the report is enough to confirm my suspicions that he is in league with the military."

"I see. And now that you have this information, what do you intend to do with it?"

"I don't know. Unless I actually discover the Unified Field Theory, it's a moot point."

"Yes, but perhaps it will prevent you from discovering it by further fueling your guilt and conflict over all of this."

Einstein nods. "I'm concerned with the discovery of knowledge. Chancellor Smith is concerned with destructive applications of that knowledge. It's very unsettling."

Einstein and Jung enter the apartment house and walk down the hall towards Pauli's apartment.

"Part of me is afraid that I won't discover the Unified Field Theory. Another part of me is afraid that I will."

Jung is about to respond to Einstein when they hear thrashing and crashing sounds coming from inside Pauli's apartment. They quickly arrive at the front door. Finding it unlocked, they enter, to find Pauli in a drunken rage.

He's overturning furniture, throwing lamps onto the floor, smashing various objects against the wall. He is totally out of control, grunting and screaming out in primal rage as he flails around the room destroying everything in his sight.

Einstein shouts, "Wolfgang!"

"Stop it!," screams Jung.

Pauli is unresponsive, continues his rampage. When Einstein and Jung try to grab him, he overpowers them, shoves them away, and runs out the door.

Einstein and Jung look at each other with a mixture of shock and deep concern.

26

Einstein and Jung are in Pauli's study. This room has also been ravaged and destroyed. Pages torn out from notebooks are scattered across the floor. On the blackboard, the number 137 and the symbol for the Greek letter Alpha are written over and over again within numerous mathematical formulas and calculations.

Jung picks up some of the loose pages from off the floor. The number 137 and the symbol for Alpha are scrawled repeatedly on these pages as well.

"What's this '137' all about?," Jung asks Einstein.

"137 is the value of Alpha, the Fine-Structure Constant," Einstein explains. "Throughout the Thirties and Forties several scientists unsuccessfully tried to discover <u>why</u> Alpha equals 137."

"It looks like Wolfgang's name can now be added to the list."

Einstein nods. "The mystery of Alpha may very well be one of those things beyond human comprehension."

"Like trying to prove the existence of God?"

"Precisely. In my opinion, the only thing Wolfgang will accomplish by obsessively tackling this problem is driving himself insane, if he hasn't done so already."

"Not that he needs much help," remarks Jung.

"What do you mean?," asks Einstein.

"Wolfgang is predisposed to insanity. His mother was a diagnosed manic-depressive. One of his sisters was institutionalized for dementia. And he was on the verge of a nervous breakdown once before."

"When his wife left him?"

"Yes. He couldn't handle the separation. He started drinking heavily. Had fits of rage. Got into several bar fights."

Einstein is incredulous. "Bar fights?!"

Jung nods. "His work failed. His lectures were incoherent. His whole life was about to self-destruct. He was having horrifying nightmares, which were tormenting him so much that he came to me for help." Jung pauses for a moment. "Ironically, it was my analysis of his nightmares which led to many of my theories on dreams, archetypes, and the Collective Unconscious. They were rich with religious symbology, much of which resembled symbols found in the Kabala, the bible of Jewish mystics."

Jung surveys the damage to the apartment and refers to it. "I pray Wolfgang did this in a drunken rage and hasn't lost touch with reality. The last time I almost didn't get him back."

27

Helen is at the stove in the kitchen, preparing a roast for an evening dinner party. Einstein, seated at the kitchen table, is helping her. He's peeling onions which are causing his eyes to water.

"You've been unusually quiet, Albert. Is there something bothering you?"

Einstein hesitates, reluctant to speak his mind. Helen notices, stops what she's doing and turns to him.

"What is it, Albert?"

"I'm going to have my machine repaired, Helen. I'm going to try using it again."

Helen reacts vehemently. "Have you lost your mind, Albert?! It almost killed you, for God's sakes!"

Einstein wipes onion tears from his eyes. "I'm sorry. I wish you could understand."

"Oh, I understand alright. You've got a death wish. There's nothing confusing about that."

"Death wish? Come on, Helen! I'm 76 years old. What does it matter if I go now or six months from now?"

Now Helen's wiping her eyes, but her tears aren't from the onions. "It matters to me."

Einstein is deeply moved by this. He wipes more onion tears from his eyes, then gets up, walks over to Helen, and puts his arms around her.

"My life has always consisted of choosing the unconventional path. I won't stop now. I can't."

"Please, Albert. Don't do this. It scares me."

Einstein smiles gently. "I'll let you in on a little secret. It scares me, too."

"Oh, Albert…"

28

Einstein, Jung, Jim Robertson and Helen are seated around the dining room table. Bertrand Russell, 70, with white hair and dark, piercing eyes glistening with intellect, enters the room.

"Glad you could make it, Bertrand," Einstein says. "I wish we could say the same for Wolfgang."

"Still no word from him?"

Einstein shakes his head no as he turns to Jung. "We might as well get started, Carl."

Jung nods, then refers to an I-Ching book which is spread open on the table in front of him.

"The I-Ching, also known as the Book of Change, is an ancient Chinese tool for acquiring wisdom and guidance. I have consulted the I-Ching hundreds of times in my life. The readings I've received have always been relevant and have often been astounding in terms of their accuracy and insight."

Jung picks up the I-Ching book and shows a page to the others, revealing a figure composed of six broken and unbroken lines.

"This is called a hexagram. The six broken and unbroken lines are produced by tossing three coins six times and recording the pattern of heads and tails. The I-Ching is an example of pure synchronicity, insofar as its hexagrams, produced by the random tossing of coins, are meaningful reflections of the universe as it's unfolding. It's not an accident the way the coins fall. The hexagrams they create are acausally connected to the questions one poses before tossing the coins.

Jung pauses. "By reading and interpreting these hexagrams, the questioner comes to know the significance of a particular moment in time, the seed from which future events blossom and flow."

Bertrand Russell interrupts Jung's discourse. "It sounds to me like you're saying that we each have a fixed destiny and are moving along a predetermined time-line. I don't buy that."

Jung shakes his head vehemently. "Divination through the I-Ching does <u>not</u> imply a pre-determined universe with a future which can be flawlessly predicted through the random tossing of three coins. No. The I-Ching exposes a moment of change in one's life, a choice point in one's life, where one's destiny is leading in <u>several</u> different directions."

Jung pauses. "The questioner uses the I-Ching to expose the various forces that are at work, so that the questioner can wisely make decisions and take actions which are in his best interests and which will lead to the ideal end result, the ideal destiny, if you will."

"The I-Ching concerns itself with probabilities," remarks Helen. "Is that what you're saying?"

Jung nods. "The I-Ching only defines the <u>moment</u>. The forces at hand <u>right now</u>. You could choose to do one thing <u>today</u>, ask the very same question <u>tomorrow</u>, and get the exact <u>opposite</u> response, depending upon the balance of forces at <u>that</u> moment in time."

"So all we can really conclude from the I-Ching," Russell says, "is that at any present moment, one particular time-line or outcome is more prevalent than the myriad others. However, by our actions, as well as the collective actions of the universe, we may or may not manifest that outcome."

Jung nods. "Nothing is etched in stone. The universe is a dynamic system, constantly in flux, contantly changing. The I-Ching provides clues. Bits of information and wisdom that can make our passage through the universe a more peaceful and harmonious journey."

An impatient Einstein interrupts. "Enough already with the talk. Let's ask the I-Ching a question."

"Very well," Jung replies. "What would you like to ask?"

Einstein reflects for a moment. "Let's ask the I-Ching what it can advise me about my work on the Unified Field Theory."

Jung nods, then takes a small coin pouch from his coat pocket and opens it. Inside the pouch are three Chinese coins, which Jung removes and hands to Einstein.

"First you must meditate briefly on your question. Then shake the coins and let them drop onto the table."

As Einstein closes his eyes and concentrates on his question, Jung takes out a pencil and notepad. After a few moments, Einstein opens his eyes, shakes the coins in his hands, and lets them fall onto the table.

Jung makes notations on his notepad as Einstein throws the coins five more times. Then he opens the I-Ching book and flips through the pages until he finds what he's looking for. He reveals a hexagram to the others:

HEXAGRAM 18

"The question was 'What can you advise me about my work on the Unified Field Theory?' And the hexagram you threw, Albert, is: 'Decay.'"

Einstein registers a look of consternation. Jung responds. "Don't be so quick to judge the answer as good or bad. Let me read you the passage... 'The object of your inquiry is in a state of disrepair. Your problems may seem to be overwhelming. Things may appear to be out of hand.'"

Einstein is startled by the accuracy of the response. "That's amazing!"

Jung nods, then continues reading. "'Yet the hexagram bodes great success. Work hard. The time is excellent for making amends. Do not discount as unimportant even the smallest detail. Do not be afraid to take assertive action. Your own past attitude has allowed the damage to occur, making you uniquely equipped to repair it. Do not be lulled into inertia by the magnitude of the task. The situation will develop new energy and inspiration as the problems are removed. Also remember that...'"

Just then, Wolfgang Pauli barges into the room. He's raving like a madman. He has a crazed, manic look in his eyes suggestive of psychotic paranoid schizophrenia. Pauli rushes up to Einstein and shouts in his face.

"Division and reduction of symmetry! This is the kernel of the brute! If only Christ and the Devil realized how they have grown so much more symmetrical! It's so simple, can't you see? It's right in front of you! Only a fool would deny the undeniable!!! The shadow world is as real as this one! Only in dreams can we escape the torment of Heaven and Hell!!!!"

Everyone looks at each other with shock and concern as Pauli continues his tirade.

"Alpha is the missing piece of the puzzle, Albert! And within it lies the secret of eternal life! But does anyone care?! Will anybody lift a finger?!! The

Devil tries to defeat me, but he will not win. The fate of all mankind hangs in the balance!!"

Pauli pauses, glares at Einstein. "Well, Professor Einstein?! What have you to say? What is your response? Come! Speak! SPEAK!!!"

"Calm down, Wolfgang. I can't understand what you're saying."

"The great Albert Einstein can't understand what I'm saying?!," Pauli exclaims derisively. "What are you, senile? It's so simple what I'm saying. A child could see it! Union is! God is! Alpha is! I AM!!"

"You are what?," asks Einstein.

"I am you! You are me! We are one!"

"What in blazes have you done to yourself?"

"I've opened my mind! Something you don't have the guts to do, you coward, you hypocrite! I've expanded my mind to encompass all of reality. Not just this reality. The reality underlying this reality!"

Einstein doesn't know what to say. "Wolfgang, I. . ."

"I took the leap, you worthless old fool! Don't you get it? There is something else! I know what is coming! I know it exactly! But I won't tell it to you! I won't tell it to anyone! That way, they'll be fooled into complacency and won't be able to perpetrate the lies."

"Who is 'they'?! What lies are you talking about?!"

"I know what is coming! I know what is coming!"

Einstein turns to Jung. "Can't you do anything for him, Carl?"

Jung shakes his head. "He's in a dissociational fugue state. He needs medication. I left my bag at home."

Pauli turns to Jung, as if seeing him in the room for the first time. Pauli points an accusatory finger at him.

"You! Traitor! Liar! Conspirator!"

Pauli lunges at Jung, grabs him by the throat. Jung's chair topples over. The two men sprawl to the floor. Pauli again clutches Jung by the throat and starts to strangle him. The others are horrified. They rush over to pull Pauli off of Jung, but in spite of the numbers being four against one, they are having great difficulty. Pauli's manic, adrenaline-pumped state has given him abnormally excessive strength and power.

"Seducer!," Pauli shrieks at Jung. "Adulterer! I'll kill you!!!"

Robertson and the others eventually succeed in pulling Pauli off of Jung, who gasps for breath and rubs his throat. Pauli continues to rave at Jung as Robertson and the others hold him down.

"You drove my wife from me. You ruined my life!!"

Jung moves closer to Pauli. "It's not true, Wolfgang. I am your friend."

"Liar! Hypocrite!"

"I have done nothing to hurt you, Wolfgang."

Jung takes Pauli's face in his hands. Whispers in a soothing, calm voice, "The truth shall set you free."

These words have a miraculous effect on Pauli. He suddenly stops raving. His body relaxes. And then he bursts into tears.

"I know what is coming," he weeps. "I know what is coming..."

And then his sobs give way to complete exhaustion. As his eyes begin to close he whispers, "I know what is coming. Perhaps I will tell you sometime..."

And then Pauli passes out. Everyone looks at each other. Totally stunned. Deeply concerned for their friend.

29

Pauli is asleep on the sofa in Einstein's study, blankets covering him. Jung and Einstein are at his side.

"I had an affair with Wolfgang's wife, Albert."

Einstein is shocked by this revelation. Jung continues. "It was two years after their divorce before I started seeing her. Their relationship was <u>definitely</u> over and done with."

"He obviously thinks that while you were counseling him you were secretly plotting to steal her away," Einstein remarks.

"It's not true, Albert."

"I know that." Einstein pauses. "How did he react to you when he initially found out about it?"

"I knew it'd be a sensitive subject that might hurt our friendship, so I never brought it up. And neither did he. So I just assumed that he didn't know or didn't care. Now I see that neither of those were true."

"Maybe not," Einstein replies.

"What do you mean?," asks Jung.

"You weren't the only one he attacked today. He threw some vicious verbal barbs my way as well. Which leads me to believe that his outbursts against <u>both</u> of us are more a reflection of his psychotic state rather than his true feelings."

"I hope you're right, Albert. This is heartbreaking to me."

"I've <u>never</u> seen Wolfgang harboring even a hint of resentment towards you, Carl. I'm sure that in his sane mind he knows you did nothing dishonorable. You'll see. One day this will all be water under the bridge."

"Assuming we can restore his sanity."

"What do you mean? There are medicines for this sort of thing, aren't there?"

"Yes, of course. But they don't always work. Every person's brain chemistry responds differently. Some people recover from an acute psychotic break. Others don't."

"My God!," Einstein exclaims. "You mean it's possible he might have to be placed in an insane asylum for the rest of his life?"

"It's possible," says Jung. "However, we do have one thing going for us."

"What's that?"

"I have my suspicions that this episode might have been chemically-induced. In which case the odds are much greater that he'll respond to treatment and recover fully."

"Chemically-induced?"

"Aldous Huxley has written a book called <u>The Doors Of Perception</u>, about his hallucinogenic experiences with mescaline. In it he describes emotional states similar to those we observed in Wolfgang."

"You <u>really</u> think that's what happened, or are you just grasping at straws?," asks Einstein.

"It's a definite possibility. I'd be even more confident that that were the case if I had some idea how Wolfgang could have gotten hold of an hallucinogenic substance."

30

Einstein and Jung are in Professor Gould's laboratory. They've just confronted him.

"Yes, I gave Professor Pauli a dose of mescaline. He said he was interested in studying its effects."

Jung is outraged by this revelation. "I find that extremely irresponsible!"

"That's not fair of you, Doctor," Professor Gould says in his defense. "I described the research I've been doing with hallucinogens. I explained to him some of the sensory states he could expect. And I warned him of the dangers. Believe me, I never would have given it to him if I thought he was emotionally unstable."

Einstein nods his understanding. "It's not your fault, Professor."

Jung gets up to leave. Einstein remains seated. Jung looks at him quizzically. "Is there something else you wish to discuss, Albert?"

"As a matter of fact there is." Einstein turns to Gould. "I would like to try a dosage of mescaline myself."

Jung's jaw drops. "What in God's name can you be thinking?!," he responds explosively. "You saw what it did to Wolfgang. Why would you want to risk that?!"

"Perhaps with a drug-induced expanded consciousness I can discover the missing pieces of my Unified Field Theory."

"That's not what this is about," replies Jung. "Wolfgang challenged you. He said you didn't have the guts to do what he did. And you need to prove him wrong. Just like one of your silly bets. This isn't about science and you know it. It's about ego."

"The mind is the final frontier. Wolfgang had the courage and the commitment to explore it, regardless of the consequences. I feel I can do no less."

"I'm against it, Albert," protests Jung. "This is foolhardy and prideful. I'm very much against it."

"I'm going to do it, Carl. That is, if Professor Gould is willing to accommodate me."

"How could I refuse Albert Einstein?"

"Thank you."

Jung is shocked. But realizing he can't talk Einstein out of it, he decides to back-pedal. "Alright, Albert. You want to take a drug and go insane, fine. At least let me be there with you, in the next room, in case something happens. Will you give me that?"

31

Einstein is at his desk in his study. He removes a tab of mescaline from a small glass vial and places it in his mouth.

A short time later, Einstein is lying on the sofa, staring up at the ceiling. His face reflects awe and amazement at the kaleidoscope of psychedelic images he's seeing.

Vibrant colors glow and pulsate incandescently. Objects in the room appear distorted as they waver and vibrate. Religious and sexual imagery flash in rapid succession, including a very quick, almost subliminal image of Einstein crucified on a cross.

All this is accompanied by the accentuated sounds of trees rustling in the wind, crickets chirping, dogs barking, cars driving down the street, and auditory hallucinations of whispering voices, words inaudible.

Einstein has a look of transcendent ecstasy on his face. When he holds his hand up in the air and stares at it, his mouth drops open in wonderment.

He can see through the skin on his hand. He can see the muscle groups. He can see the nerves. He can see the blood vessels pulsing. He can see the blood coursing through his arteries and veins.

Einstein gets up and walks over to the mirror on the wall. He looks at himself in the mirror. His face appears distorted. And then something remarkable happens. His face starts changing right before his eyes. Various animal faces are rapidly superimposed over his human countenance, ending with the face of a wild, prehistoric cro-magnon man. The face suddenly growls, and appears to come out of the mirror, towards Einstein, just like in a 3-D movie.

Einstein jumps back and away from the mirror with a shout of fear and horror. As he catches his breath, Jung barges through the door in response to Einstein's yell.

"Are you alright, Albert?"

Einstein nods.

"My face... prehistoric man..." He pauses. "I'm <u>seeing</u> sounds!... <u>tasting</u> colors!... intricacies... subtleties... nature... life... death... love... hate... war... peace... fearless... wholeness... one-ness... unity... <u>God</u>!"

Einstein looks at Jung for his response. And nearly has a heart attack when Jung dematerializes right before his eyes. Just disappears! Evaporates! Einstein was talking to an hallucination!

"Carl!... CARL!!," Einstein shouts.

Within moments, Jung barges into the room, just like his hallucination did a few moments before, and says the very same thing his hallucination said to Einstein.

"Are you alright, Albert?"

Einstein looks at him closely, reaches out and touches his shoulder. Feels the substantive nature of Jung's body.

Einstein is awestruck. "Incredible! <u>Just</u> <u>incredible</u>!"

32

Einstein and Helen are sitting in the rocking chairs on the porch of Einstein's house.

"It was an incredible experience, Helen. Think about it. If Carl's body ap-peared to exist but wasn't really there, then perhaps everything that fills the space we live in is also an illusion."

"This rocking chair is no illusion, Albert. It's solid. It isn't going to suddenly disappear."

"Perhaps it is merely a more complex illusion. Perhaps on some other level of perception, on some other plane of existence, this chair, this whole planet is immaterial."

Helen looks at Einstein askance. "I don't know about this, Albert."

Einstein continues, unfazed. "If that's the premise, that physical time and space as we know it are elaborate illusions, then any Unified Field Theory hop-ing to explain the way the universe works must inherently have a variable or a constant that takes into account this illusory and transcendent aspect. Which means that I've got to go beyond a three-dimensional Theory of Relativity. I've got to start thinking in terms of a multi-dimensional Theory of Relativity that goes beyond my present, limited perspective of time and space."

Helen stares at Albert with a skeptical and concerned expression on her face. "Are you sure you're not experiencing any residual effects from that drug you took?"

Einstein chuckles. "I'm fine, Helen. And I've never been thinking more clearly in my life." He pauses. "Up to now I've fixated on a time-space model which <u>isn't</u> valid. How could I hope to find an answer when my question was improperly conceptualized? I couldn't! But now, with this expanded understanding of the insubstantiality of time and space, I have a chance to re-formulate the equations and perhaps solve the puzzle once and for all."

33

Einstein is having his recurring underwater nightmare. He's at the bottom of the ocean, holding his breath, frantically swimming upward toward the light at the surface. But no matter how hard and fast he swims, he can't seem to get any closer to the top.

**

Einstein, Pauli and Jung are sitting on the deck of Einstein's sailboat as it glides across Carnegie Lake. It's a magnificent day with beautiful blue skies and billowy white clouds.

Pauli appears drugged and sedated. "I'm tired all the time," he complains. "My thoughts are fuzzy and diffuse. I can't think. I can't work. How long must I keep taking this medication?"

"Another week or two, Wolfgang," replies Jung.

Pauli groans in protest.

"It won't be as bad as it is now," Jung continues. "Starting today I'll be gradually reducing the dosage. You'll feel more and more like your old self with each passing day."

Pauli nods. "Very well."

Jung turns to Einstein. "Now then, Albert, tell us your dream."

"It's the same one I had a few weeks ago," Einstein begins. "<u>Exactly</u> the same. I'm underwater, trying to swim up to the surface where the light is, but no matter how hard I try, I can't seem to make any headway. Just as my lungs are about to burst, I wake up."

"Your dream reflects your struggle with the Unified Field Theory," explains Jung. "Your difficulty getting to the surface where the light is — where the answer is — represents the resistance you're still hanging onto."

"Makes sense," Einstein says.

Jung nods. "Psychologists working with the Senoi tribe in Africa have formulated a new dream theory called 'Lucid Dreaming.' They claim it's possible to bring your conscious mind into the dream state and direct your dream self to overcome the dream obstacle. And that if you do this, you will essentially be defeating the obstacle in your <u>real</u> life which the dream obstacle symbolizes." He pauses. "Have I totally confused you?"

Einstein shakes his head no. "You're saying that if I can direct the outcome of my dream, I will be sending the message to my subconscious mind that I'm ready to take responsibility for the direction of my life and the consequences of my actions. I'll basically be releasing whatever fear or guilt is causing my subconscious mind to resist my conscious mind's desire for success."

"Precisely," smiles Jung.

34

Einstein is working in his Princeton University office when he hears a knock on the door. "Yes?," Einstein calls out.

Chancellor Smith enters. "May I have a moment of your time, Albert?"

"Come in. Have a seat."

Chancellor Smith sits down.

"What is it you wish to speak to me about?," Einstein asks the Chancellor.

"I'm concerned about you, Albert. You've been looking very tired lately."

Einstein reacts instantly and with hostility. "Stop it! You're not concerned about me. You're concerned about my work and if I'll live long enough to produce the ultimate formula for a weapon of mass destruction which you can deliver to the war machine in Washington."

Chancellor Smith shakes his head. "Is there nothing I can say to assure you that I share your humanistic concerns about the applications of any theory you may develop?"

"That depends. Is there anything you can say to assure me that the Pentagon's 'Advanced Weapons Systems Program' is designed to promote harmony, good will, and peace on Earth?"

Chancellor Smith is shocked by Einstein's knowledge of the Pentagon weapons program, but masks his surprise. "What weapons program? I don't know what you're talking about."

Einstein chuckles. "Of course you don't. How foolish of me. Forgive me. I'm just a senile old man." Einstein pauses. "Is there anything else you wanted to discuss?"

Chancellor Smith shakes his head no.

"In that case, if you'll excuse me, I have work to do."

Einstein returns to his work. A very displeased Chancellor Smith gets up and exits the office.

35

Einstein is sitting at his desk in his study at home, staring at his little machine which has been repaired. He hesitates for a few beats, gathers up his courage, and then straps it on his head.

Einstein flips the "on" switch. The headpiece starts humming. The humming gets louder. And then he hears a high-pitched whine that also gets louder until something shocking happens:

The study begins blinking on and off, dissolving in and out periodically. Each dissolve lasts a very brief time interval. And in those dissolves, Einstein sees another physical reality blinking on and off, dissolving in and out in its place:

It's Einstein's 1919 Berlin bedroom. And there as plain as day is 40-Year-Old Einstein sitting up in bed!

76-Year-Old Einstein's face registers absolute amazement and awe! After a few moments he turns off the machine. As his reality returns to normal, he contemplates the significance of this phenomenal experience.

**

Einstein sits at his piano in his study, lost in thought as he taps away at the keyboard, improvising a melancholic tune. His reverie is broken by a knock at the door.

"Come in."

Helen enters. She holds a manuscript in her hand and has an excited expression on her face.

"Listen to this, Albert!" Helen reads from the manuscript. "'Resonance of quantum wave frequencies would create a superimposition of the past onto the present, in which both worlds would be observed simultaneously.'"

Einstein responds with great excitement. "That's what was happening! Except that the two wave frequencies were out of synch. So instead of a true superimposition, I perceived an alternation of realities!"

Einstein pauses. Refers to Helen's manuscript. "Who wrote that?"

"A grad student. Hugh Everett."

**

Einstein and Hugh Everett, a man in his thirties with an intellectual demeanor and a twinkle in his eye, are having a conversation in Einstein's study. Everett is explaining his theory.

"The past and the future are here right now, all around us, but in other dimensions, other reality frequencies, if you will. And, someday, when the human brain has evolved to a more advanced state, man will be able to use his mind to tune into these other realities."

36

Einstein is asleep at his desk in his study. Notebooks with calculations are scattered all around him. He's having his recurring underwater nightmare again.

**

Einstein is at the bottom of the ocean, holding his breath, frantically swimming upward toward the light at the surface. But no matter how hard and fast he swims, he doesn't seem to be getting any closer to the top.

This time, however, instead of waking up, he speaks to himself while in the dream state.

"This is a dream. I can control the outcome. I can overcome my conflicts and my fears. I can rise to the surface now."

And with those words, Einstein's dream body instantly bursts upward from underwater, into the light of day. It's a beautiful, balmy day with blue skies. Einstein's dream body floats on top of the water, basking in the warmth of the sun.

**

Einstein wakes up from his dream. Instead of being in torment, his face now reflects relief and serenity.

As he raises his head off of the desk, the first thing he sees is his little machine sitting on top of the bookcase.

He wryly quips to himself, "No time like the present."

**

It's 1919. 40-Year-Old Einstein opens up a hat box in his Berlin apartment, pulls out his little machine, places it on his head, and flips the "on" switch.

At the exact same time, 76-Year-Old Einstein flips the "on" switch on the headpiece that he's wearing in his 1955 Princeton study.

The result is an awesome explosion of blinding light. And then the two realities – 40-Year-Old Einstein's 1919 study and 76-Year-Old Einstein's 1955 study – begin alternating, blinking on and off, one dissolving into the other, over and over again, just as it happened earlier.

Only this time they are alternating at an ever-accelerating rate, accompanied by an ever-accelerating high-pitched whine.

This is followed by a sonic boom! And another explosion of blinding white light!

And the result of this "reality collision" is a "composite reality" made up of Einstein's 1919 study and Einstein's 1955 study, one superimposed over the other. The result is a weird mosaic of the two rooms. Each with its own Einstein.

40-Year-Old Einstein and 76-Year-Old Einstein stare at each other in awe. The 76-Year-Old Einstein is amazed, but not totally taken aback by this, insofar as he was desensitized by his earlier experience with the two realities blinking on and off. The 40-Year-Old Einstein, on the other hand, is completely taken by surprise.

"You're... ?!"

76-Year-Old Einstein nods. "Albert Einstein."

"I'm Albert Einstein!," 40-Year-Old Einstein protests.

76-Year-Old Einstein grins. "Yes, I know. Pleased to see you again."

40-Year-Old Einstein is fascinated. "This is an incredible hallucination!"

"I am no hallucination," 76-Year-Old Einstein says with a twinkle in his eye. "At least no more than you are."

40-Year-Old Einstein laughs. "What a delightful development!"

76-Year-Old Einstein reiterates firmly, "I am <u>not</u> an hallucination! I am you. In the year 1955. At the age of 76 years old."

40-Year-Old Einstein laughs. "Impossible!"

"No! This 'impossibility' is reality! We <u>made </u>this happen with our little machines."

40-Year-Old Einstein is still skeptical.

"Look at the clocks," insists 76-Year-Old Einstein.

40-Year-Old Einstein looks first at his clock. It has stopped at 2:22. Then 40-Year-Old Einstein looks at 76-Year-Old Einstein's clock. It, too, has stopped at 2:22.

"So the clocks stopped at the same time," says 40-Year-Old Einstein. "That proves this is not an hallucinatory experience induced by my little machine? I don't think so."

76-Year-Old Einstein is frustrated with his younger self. "You turned your machine on at the same time I turned my machine on. And somehow the time-space matrix was altered. Don't you see?! Time travel is no longer theoretical. We have opened the door linking both our worlds – your time and mine."

"Prove it! <u>Prove</u> that this isn't an hallucination. <u>Prove</u> that you're from the future. Can you do that?"

76-Year-Old Einstein reflects on this challenge for a moment. Then he pats his pants' pockets and hears a tinkling sound. A smile appears on his face as he reaches into his pocket and triumphantly removes several coins. He holds them out for 40-Year-Old Einstein, who takes them, and examines them closely.

As 40-Year-Old Einstein checks the dates on the coins, his face reflects the awe and wonderment accompanying his realization.

"This is incredible!," 40-Year-Old Einstein shouts. "Time and space no longer exist as we know it!"

76-Year-Old Einstein grins. "Correct."

40-Year-Old Einstein looks around at the composite room. "It seems that we've done more than link both our worlds. We've gone <u>beyond</u> time and space. We're in another place entirely."

76-Year-Old Einstein nods. "A <u>composite</u> world in its own time-space frequency."

"Hmm," says 40-Year-Old Einstein. "Kind of like the multiple realities and parallel universes of science fiction."

"It's not science fiction anymore," smiles 76-Year-Old Einstein.

"So what do we do now?"

76-Year-Old Einstein shrugs. "Is there anything you'd like to know about the future?"

40-Year-Old Einstein considers this for a moment. "A consequence of the Theory of Relativity is the concept of atomic clocks. Have they been invented?"

"Yes. International Time is now regulated by atomic clocks. And engineers are now developing laser technology, also based on our theories, which will have major applications in research, medicine, and industry."

"How wonderful!"

"Yes, that's true." He pauses sadly. "But you don't know the grief, the suffering, the death that has resulted from our Theory of Relativity as well."

"What do you mean?"

"Atomic bombs," 76-Year-Old Einstein says somberly. "They were dropped on the Japanese people at the end of World War II."

"World War II?"

"Hundreds of thousands of people dead in a matter of seconds. And unborn generations carrying a devastating genetic legacy."

"My God!," 40-Year-Old Einstein exclaims.

"And now mankind lives in perpetual fear," 76-year-old Einstein continues. "A nuclear albatross eternally hanging around its neck."

40-Year-Old Einstein is numb. "To be responsible for the deaths of hundreds of thousands of people. I never dreamed it would happen."

One would expect 76-Year-Old Einstein to agree with his younger counterpart. But instead, something unexpected happens. An awareness that has been struggling for attention and acceptance in his consciousness finally succeeds in taking root and transforming his attitude. His guilt-ridden angst washes from his countenance. His life-long conflict is finally resolved as he defends his past where before he was apologizing for it.

"We aren't responsible! We didn't create those bombs! We discovered the truth and gave it to the world. Period! It was others who took the truth, who took the knowledge, and applied it towards weaponry and destruction. We discovered laws of nature. We did not invent atomic weapons."

As 40-Year-Old Einstein digests the passionate argument he has just heard, 76-Year-Old Einstein is also processing it, and comes to another conclusion.

"Carl was right. I've been blocking the discovery of the Unified Field Theory because of my obsession with the atomic bomb. Because of guilt."

"And just now, talking to me, you realized that you needn't feel guilty for the past anymore?"

76-Year-Old Einstein nods. "Or for a possible future. I needn't fear discovery of the Unified Field Theory anymore. After all, man tries to turn <u>everything</u> into a weapon. So to resist scientific progress on the basis of man's eternal potential for violence would serve only to honor ignorance, darkness and fear. In its pure and absolute state as a law of universal action, the Unified Field Theory can <u>only</u> be a blessing."

"I don't know if I agree with that. I'm not convinced that the truth is such a wonderful gift to mankind if death is the price to be paid. I think it might have been better if we had been a plumber instead."

76-Year-Old Einstein shakes his head no. "Our commitment has always been to the discovery of knowledge and truth, to the discovery of <u>cause</u>, not <u>effects</u>. We must stay true to that commitment." He pauses. "I wish <u>all</u> my doubts were as easily resolved as this one."

"What do you mean?"

"My celebrity status gave me a voice to the people of the world. An opportunity to influence future generations."

"And you think you failed in this? Misused that voice?"

"I waffled," 76-Year-Old Einstein sighs. "I reversed my pacifist position."

"What?! Why?!," a shocked 40-Year-Old Einstein asks.

"A fascist named Adolf Hitler came into power in Germany. He was responsible for the murder of millions of innocent people. Amidst that, I could not stay true to my absolute pacifist stance on non-violence and non-cooperation." 76-Year-Old Einstein sighs. "My stance against nationalism? When put to the test, I flip-flopped on that one, too."

"What happened?"

"I supported the formation of a Jewish nation. For the same reason that I advocated force and aggression against Hitler. I feared for the annihilation of my people."

76-Year-Old Einstein pauses thoughtfully for a moment. "Both cases were exceptions after which I reverted back to my former stance."

40-Year-Old Einstein lets this sink in for a few seconds. And then:

"Even with your exceptions, you still advocated magnificent ideals, which I am sure left an impact on people, made them think, question their beliefs, and discuss their ideas with others. That you weren't perfect is no reason to negate all the good that you accomplished."

40-Year-Old Einstein moves to his bookshelf. "And besides, remember what Ralph Waldo Emerson once said? 'A foolish consistency is the hobgoblin of little minds.'"

40-Year-Old Einstein pulls out a book, opens it at a bookmark, looks at the bookmark and laughs. He holds it up for his counterpart to see. "A check I never deposited."

40-Year-Old Einstein and 76-Year-Old Einstein share a knowing chuckle. And then 40-Year-Old Einstein finds a specific passage in the book he's holding.

"Here we go." He reads aloud from the book. "'Speak what you think now in hard words and tomorrow speak what tomorrow thinks in hard words again, though it may contradict everything you said today. Ah, so you shall be sure to be misunderstood? Pythagoras was misunderstood, and Socrates, and Jesus, and Luther, and Copernicus, and Galileo, and Newton, and every pure and wise spirit that ever took flesh. To be great is to be misunderstood.'"

76-Year-Old Einstein ponders the words for a moment, nods in appreciation. "Thank you."

Just then 40-Year-Old Einstein's little machine starts shorting-out, and smoke starts spewing from the top of it. The composite world the two Einsteins are sharing starts to vibrate, the high-pitched whine we heard before starts up again.

"Our composite world is becoming unstable," says 40-Year-Old Einstein. "We're about to go our separate ways."

"But we've only just gotten started. There's still so much to talk about."

"I'll fix the short in my machine," 40-Year-Old Einstein says. "We'll do this again."

"But how can we guarantee that we'll again synchronize both worlds?," 76-Year-Old Einstein asks his younger self.

"We can't. The best we can do is turn our machines on at exactly 2:22, just like we did this time."

"Agreed."

And then there is a flash of blinding white light!

**

40-Year-Old Einstein lies unconscious on the floor in his Berlin apartment. The little machine on his head is smoking. His eyes open. His expression reflects no awareness of what has transpired.

He looks at his clock. It reads 2:22. Not a second has passed. Einstein smells the smoke coming from his headpiece. Turns it off, removes it, and examines the wires that shorted out.

"<u>Damn</u>!" Then he shrugs. "Oh well. Nothing ventured, nothing gained. I'll fix it and try again."

**

In his Princeton house, 76-Year-Old Einstein takes his little machine off his head. He remembers <u>everything</u> that has just happened. He looks at his clock. It's 2:22. Not a second has passed.

"Where does the time go?," he chuckles.

37

Einstein and Jung are driving in a car, talking about Pauli.

"Wolfgang stopped taking his medication, Albert. He went to a bar and began drinking heavily. Then he started smashing glasses on the floor while raving about 137 being the master number of the Kabala."

Einstein shakes his head in disbelief. "How's he doing now?"

"He's okay. The police brought him to the hospital to dry out for a few days."

"Is 137 the master number of the Kabala?," Einstein asks Jung.

"Yes. I checked it this morning."

"How bizarre is that, that 137 is Alpha, the Fine-Structure Constant, and the master number in an ancient philosophy of Jewish mystics?"

"You haven't heard the wildest part."

"What's that?"

"The hospital room they stuck Wolfgang in? Are you ready for this? Room number 137."

"You can't be serious."

"It's true."

"That's a very impressive coincidence."

Jung nods knowingly. "Synchronicty strikes again!"

38

Pauli is sitting up in a hospital bed. Einstein and Jung are sitting in chairs beside him. Einstein has been describing his experience with his little machine.

"If it really happened, Albert, why don't you remember it happening to you when you were forty years old?," Jung asks Einstein.

"I see what you're saying," Einstein replies. "Maybe I did hallucinate it."

Pauli shakes his head. "No, Albert. If it did happen, which it could have, your younger self should have forgotten it."

"Why?," asks Jung.

"Are we in agreement that time is an illusion?," Pauli begins. The others nod yes. "And are we in agreement that the past, present and future are all happening right now?"

Einstein and Jung again nod their agreement.

"Then the reason why your younger self didn't remember the experience he had is the same reason why we don't remember the <u>future</u> now."

"I don't follow," says Jung.

"The human mind, for whatever reason, has given an <u>arrow</u> to time," Pauli continues. "A direction from past to future. We remember the past. We don't remember the future. So 76-Year-Old Einstein remembers the experience, but 40-Year-Old Einstein does not."

"Interesting," says Einstein. "But if it did happen and I want it to happen again – if my younger self doesn't remember our conversation, how will we be able to synchronize our efforts?"

"Since all time is simultaneous, since everything is happening now... if your younger self puts on his machine and you put on yours, it will, by definition, be happening simultaneously and the two worlds will coincide."

39

Einstein is asleep. He's dreaming. In his dream, he is treking across a mountain, in the middle of a blizzard, battling vicious winds and blinding snow.

Eventually he breaks through the blizzard and arrives at the top of the mountain. He is above the storm which continues to rage below him.

In the distance he sees a clearing. In the clearing are a table and two chairs. Einstein walks over to them and sees a chessboard with chess pieces on the table. A game is in progress.

Einstein sits in one of the chairs, stares down at the chessboard and surveys the pieces. After a few moments, he looks up and sees his younger self, 40-Year-Old Einstein, wearing mechanics overalls, walking toward him, carrying an apple pie.

When 40-Year-Old Einstein reaches 76-Year-Old Einstein, he points to the chessboard. "It's your move."

76-Year-Old Einstein quickly glances at the chess pieces, then picks up his bishop and moves it to another position. 40-Year-Old Einstein smiles warmly at him, then cuts a slice of the apple pie and hands it to him.

"Here. Take a bite," says 40-Year-Old Einstein.

76-Year-Old Einstein hesitates, then takes a bite of the apple pie. It's bitter. He spits it out.

"You must eat it!," shouts 40-Year-Old Einstein adamantly. "Or the game will never end!"

76-Year-Old Einstein gets up from the table, takes the pie in his hand and throws it over the edge of the mountain. To his surprise and dismay, the pie falls up! This terrifies him. He lets out a gut-wrenching, tortured primal scream. And with that he wakes up from his dream.

40

Einstein and Jung are in the sailboat, sailing peacefully across Carnegie Lake. It's a beautiful sunny day.

"So what do you make of my dream, Carl?"

"The mountaintop suggests to me that Higher Intelligence is what you seek. The clearing above the blizzard suggests the calm clarity of the Collective Unconscious. The chess game symbolizes the Unified Field Theory your conscious mind is struggling with."

"Sounds reasonable."

"Now then," Jung continues. "What about your younger self wearing mechanics overalls?"

Einstein reflects for a moment and then it hits him. "Quantum Mechanics!"

"Good! And his serving you the apple pie?"

"When he told me that I've got to eat the pie or the game will never end, he was talking about Quantum Mechanics. That I've got to accept it if I'm ever going to get beyond it!"

"Interesting. Why apple pie?"

"I don't know."

"What does the word pie make you think of?"

Einstein searches his mind. "Pie… pie…" And then it occurs to him: "<u>Of course</u>! The constant <u>pi</u>! By serving me pie, I was telling myself that pi is part of the answer. One of the hidden variables!"

"And what do you associate with the word apple?"

"Apple… apple… Adam's apple."

"What do you think of when you think of Adam?"

"The first man."

"What do you associate with 'first'?"

"First… first… <u>Alpha</u>! The Fine-structure Constant! It must be part of the equation as well!" Einstein chuckles with delight. "Wolfgang's going to love that!"

"You said you moved one of the chess pieces."

"Yes. A bishop."

"What do you associate with the word bishop?"

"Clergy."

"Go on. Free associate."

"Religion… God… The Cosmos…"

His face suddenly reacts, but he stops short of speaking. Jung picks up on it. "What were you just thinking?," he asks Einstein.

"I was thinking of the Cosmological Constant."

"What's that?"

"In a paper published in 1919, entitled 'Cosmological Considerations on the General Theory of Relativity,' I introduced into my equations a universal constant. I called it the Cosmological Constant and defined it as a force which counteracts the effect of gravity between galaxies."

"Why did you not say it when it occurred to you just now?"

"The Cosmological Constant was a mistake. I was initially prompted to introduce it into my equations because I thought I had discovered a loophole in my Theory of Relativity when it depicted an expanding rather than a static universe. When Professor Hubble showed that the universe was indeed expanding, I <u>regretted</u> tinkering with my equation and publicly disclaimed and refuted the Cosmological Constant as unnecessary and unjustified. So the symbol in the dream has to mean something else because the Cosmological Constant just isn't valid."

Jung sits quietly for a beat and then continues his dream analysis. "In your dream, you said you threw the pie off the mountain, but instead of falling down, it fell up."

"Yes, that's true. So?"

"Apple falls up… anti-gravity…"

"…The Cosmological Constant," muses Einstein. "I see what you mean. But I still don't believe it's part of the equation. The pie falling up has to mean something else."

41

A torrential thunderstorm is pelting against the large window in Einstein's study as Einstein picks up his little machine, places it on his head, and turns it on. It starts humming. This is followed by a high-pitched whine, which accelerates to near-deafening proportions.

The blinking on-and-off phenomenon again occurs in which 76-year-old Einstein's world dissolves in and out periodically.

But this time, instead of Einstein's 40-Year-Old world dissolving in and out in its place, other worlds blink in and out instead: parallel worlds with parallel Einsteins. Each world and each Einstein different, because of different choices made:

76-Year-Old Einstein with an elderly Elsa by his side. (She didn't die in this parallel world.)

76-Year-Old Einstein working in his office at the University of Berlin instead of Princeton University. (There was no Hitler in this parallel world to drive Einstein out of Germany.)

Wolfgang Pauli and Carl Jung, both in their 40s, attending Einstein's funeral. (In this parallel world, Einstein put on his little machine and was electrocuted, dying instantly.)

40-Year-Old Einstein in plumbler's garb, working on a sink. (He never became a physicist in this parallel world.)

The last parallel world that blinks on and off contains the 40-Year-Old Einstein from Einstein's past in his 1919 Berlin apartment. His little machine has been repaired. He places it on his head and turns it on.

It starts humming. The high-pitched whine accelerates. This is followed by a blinding flash of white light.

And then there it is again: The composite study consisting of 40-Year-Old Einstein's Berlin study and 76-Year-Old Einstein's Princeton study.

The thunderstorm is still booming and crackling and pelting rain outside the window in the composite study as 40-Year-Old Einstein and 76-Year-Old Einstein stand face-to-face once again.

This is old news for 76-Year-Old Einstein. But for 40-Year-Old Einstein, who doesn't remember the first experience they shared together, this is a brand-new event. He reacts <u>exactly</u> the same way he did previously.

"You're... ?!," he exclaims.

76-Year-Old Einstein nods, "Albert Einstein."

"I'm Albert Einstein!"

76-Year-Old Einstein grins. "Yes, I know. Pleased to see you again."

40-Year-Old Einstein is fascinated. "This is an <u>incredible</u> hallucination!"

"I am no hallucination," 76-Year-Old Einstein replies with a twinkle in his eye. "At least no more than you are."

**

A short time later, 76-Year-Old Einstein has finished explaining to his younger counterpart that this is not an hallucination. They have begun discussing theoretical issues that they didn't get to the last time they were together.

"What if there is a smaller unit of energy that hasn't been discovered yet?," asks 76-Year-Old Einstein. "An invisible unit of energy that, when combined with similar units, reaches a threshold and manifests itself in physical terms."

"Pure energy without mass," responds 40-Year-Old Einstein. "The energy of <u>Mind</u>. Of <u>consciousness</u>."

76-Year-Old Einstein pauses to consider this new line of thought. "If time and space are illusions, then it's all got to start somewhere. Perhaps these 'Consciousness Units' are the catalysts, the building blocks for everything that exists in our physical universe!"

40-Year-Old Einstein's eyes light up as a revelation hits him. "<u>Consciousness Units</u>! <u>Yes</u>! <u>That's it</u>! That plugs up the loophole I've been worried about in the Theory of Relativity!"

"No," 76-Year-Old Einstein says softly.

Absorbed in his thoughts, 40-Year-Old Einstein doesn't hear 76-Year-Old Einstein's objection. He continues his line of reasoning: "A <u>Cosmological Constant</u>! Defined in terms of Consciousness Units. And representing a universal anti-gravity force which serves as a cosmic glue! Thus resolving the issue of a static versus an expanding universe!" He's exhilarated. "This is <u>fantastic</u>!"

"No, no, no!," 76-Year-Old Einstein insists. "The Cosmological Constant isn't the answer. I thought it was, too, when I was your age. But I regretted it years later and refuted its validity." He shakes his head vehemently. "No, it's not the answer. It's…"

And then an amazing realization occurs to him. "My God! I was wrong! The Cosmological Constant is the answer you've been seeking. And, oddly enough, it's also the pivotal answer <u>I've</u> been seeking as well! This is unbelievable! It's been in plain sight for over 36 years, but I was looking at it the <u>wrong way</u>. <u>That's</u> why the apple pie in my dream went up instead of down! The Cosmological Constant is valid. It is part of the Unified Field Theory!" He grins. "How ironic and marvelous that it is <u>myself</u> – <u>you</u> – that finally reveals the secret to me!"

"I don't understand," says 40-Year-Old Einstein.

But before 76-Year-Old Einstein can respond, a lightning bolt crashes through the window and splits into two bolts, one hitting 40-Year-Old Einstein's little machine, the other hitting 76-Year-Old Einstein's little machine! And with that there is a burst of blinding white light.

**

40-Year-Old Einstein lies unconscious on the floor in his 1919 Berlin apartment. His eyes slowly open. He stands up and removes his little machine from his head. It's charred and destroyed, smoke is emanating from the fused and fried electrical wires and circuitry.

Again, he remembers nothing about the experience he's just shared with his counterpart. Shrugging his shoulders, he moves to his desk and places the machine in the hat box, then puts the hat box in the closet with other junk and paraphernalia he's collected over the years.

**

76-Year-Old Einstein lies unconscious on the floor in his 1955 Princeton study. His eyes open. He slowly gets up. Without taking his charred and destroyed little machine off of his head, he rushes over to his desk, sits down, and starts working feverishly on his calculations, talking to himself as he does so.

"It's not <u>solely</u> an anti-gravity force. That was my problem, fixating on that aspect alone. In some cases the Cosmological Constant must <u>combine</u> with gravity, rather than counteracting its effects. Yes, that's got to be it!"

Einstein makes a final notation, then looks at the formula on the notepad before him. He seems pleased at first, but then his expression changes to a grimace.

"<u>Damn</u>! There's <u>still</u> something missing! But <u>what</u>??"

42

Pauli is in bed in the hospital. He doesn't look well. Jung and Einstein sit beside him.

"And then a series of parallel worlds started flashing before my eyes!," Einstein explains. "In one world I was a plumber. In another world, Elsa was still alive."

"Parallel worlds all happening at once!," Pauli says excitedly.

Jung chimes in, "It's mind-boggling!"

And then something occurs to Einstein. A great revelation.

"Oh my God!" He pauses. "<u>Now</u> the 'Cat In The Box' experiment makes sense!"

"What do you mean?," asks Pauli.

"It's not a question of a cat in an inbetween state, neither alive nor dead until we open the box and look inside. And it's not a question of a live cat or a dead cat inside the box waiting to be discovered. There is a live cat <u>and</u> a dead cat! <u>Both</u> exist. But in <u>different worlds</u>! When you open the box in <u>this</u> world and find a live cat, a parallel world is <u>instantly created</u> containing the alternate possibility, a dead cat in the box."

Pauli catches on. "And if <u>all</u> possibilities splinter off into their own separate worlds, if <u>all events happen</u>, then there's no random action! Therefore..."

Einstein completes the thought. "... the uncertainty at our uni-dimensional level is, in reality, part of a greater plan of certainty at the Many-Worlds level."

"So it is our <u>choice</u> that decides which world we inhabit. Not chance," says Pauli. "You were right, Albert."

Einstein nods and chuckles with delight. "I was right. God does not play dice with the universe!"

"Outrageous!," exclaims Jung.

"Not only is it outrageous," says Einstein. "It's a critical and key element of the universe which <u>must</u> be integrated into the Unified Field Theory formula for the formula to have any validity!"

"I think I know how you can do that," says Pauli.

"How?"

"By expressing it as a coefficient of the Cosmological Constant."

This excites Einstein. "An <u>excellent</u> idea, Wolfgang!"

Jung looks at his two friends with great joy and love. All three men are ecstatically happy. Jung gets up, goes to the bedside table and pours three glasses of water from a water pitcher. He hands a glass to Pauli and a glass to Einstein, then picks up the third glass and raises it in the air.

"To truth!"

The three friends pick up their glasses, just as they did 36 years before. And in unison they exclaim, "To truth!"

43

A dinner party is in progress. Einstein, Helen, Jung, and Bertrand Russell are seated around the dining room table engaged in conversation.

"Tell me something, Albert," says Jung. "Do you think the current atomic armaments race will lead to another World War or, as some people believe, act as a means to prevent war?"

"Armaments are no protection against war. Real peace <u>cannot</u> be reached without systematic disarmament on a supra-national scale, which means that mankind must transcend its nationalistic fervor in favor of a <u>supra</u>-national organization. One World. A Brotherhood of people. Everyone responsible for each other."

"But isn't it possible to prepare for war <u>and</u> a world community at the same time?," asks Jung.

Einstein is vehement on this point. "Striving for peace and preparing for war are <u>incompatible</u> with each other."

Bertrand Russell enters the discussion. "Yes, but can we really <u>ever</u> prevent war from happening?"

"If we have the courage to decide for peace, we will have peace," says Einstein. "If we are not firmly decided to resolve things in a peaceful way, we will never come to a peaceful solution."

"In the meantime," says Jung, "it's a frighteningly real possibility that in any future World War, nuclear weapons will be used, jeopardizing all life on the planet."

Bertrand Russell nods in agreement. "Schools are out to teach patriotism. Newspapers are out to stir up excitement. And politicians are out to get re-elected. None of them, therefore, will do anything whatsoever toward saving the race from reciprocal suicide."

"The scientists must do it, Bertrand," says Einstein. "We, whose tragic destiny it has been to help make the methods of annihilation ever more gruesome and effective, must do all in our power to prevent these weapons from ever being used."

"I agree," says Russell. "We must make a plea to the leaders of the world to find peaceful means for the settlement of all matters of dispute between them. A Pacifist Manifesto signed by scientists and scholars."

"An excellent idea," remarks Jung. "But what can a private individual do about peace?"

Einstein has the answer to this one. "Individuals can cause anyone who tries to be elected to public office to give a clear promise to work for international order. And insofar as everyone is involved in forming public opinion, each person must understand the issues and have the courage to speak out."

Suddenly, Einstein's face scrunches up. His whole body contorts in response to an intense paroxysm of pain. He yells out. His hands clutch his chest. He gasps. And then slumps forward, unconscious.

Helen screams, "<u>Albert</u>!"

44

Einstein's body lies motionless in a hospital bed. He's attached to tubes and machines. Doctor Dean stands beside Helen at Einstein's bedside.

"There's no way of knowing if he'll come out of the coma or not. I'm sorry, Helen."

Doctor Dean exits the room, leaving a distraught Helen alone with the comatose Einstein. Helen stares at him for a beat, her eyes filling with tears. Then she picks a book up from the bedside table, opens it, and begins reading aloud from it, her voice cracking with emotion and heartache.

"'Lives of great men all remind us, we can make our lives sublime, and, departing, leave behind us footprints on the sands of time. Footprints, that perhaps another, sailing o'er life's solemn main, a forlorn and shipwrecked brother, seeing, shall take heart again.'" She pauses for a moment and then continues reading. "'Let us then be up and doing. With a heart for any fate. Still achieving, still pursuing. Learn to labor and to wait.'"

Helen closes the book. She leans into Einstein and gives him a gentle kiss on the forehead. Then she sits down in the chair to begin her all-night vigil.

**

It's the following morning. Einstein lies unconscious in bed. Helen sits across from him. She's been up all night. Her heartache is painfully evident. Suddenly

Einstein's eyes flutter and open. Helen jumps out of her chair and gives him a big hug.

**

Later that day, Einstein is sitting up in bed. Helen, his son Hans Albert, and his granddaughter Elsa are at his side.

"I caught the first plane out," says Hans Albert.

"Thank you. I'm glad you're here, son."

The warmth of the moment is interrupted by Doctor Dean's entrance. He has a somber look on his face. Before he can utter a word, Einstein interjects.

"The truth, Doctor."

Doctor Dean pauses for a moment before speaking. "There is nothing more we can do. The aneurysm will rupture beyond repair in the very near future."

Helen gasps. Hans Albert pales. Einstein appears stoical and calm. "How long do I have?"

"A week. Maybe less."

Hans Albert and Helen are a lot more shaken by the news than is Einstein. They both look devastated. He doesn't.

"Enough of all this morbidness," he insists. "Let me tell you a joke I heard… This little old Jewish lady is at the airport ticket counter. 'I vant a ticket to India,' she says. 'I vant to see the Guru.' The ticket person says it's very expensive and very difficult to reach the Guru. He lives way high up in the Himalayas and is very inaccessible. She says, 'I vant to see the Guru.' So she gets a ticket and flies to India. She goes to a tour guide and asks to be taken up into the Himalayas to the Guru. She is told that it is very treacherous and that there's no guarantee that she will find him. She says, 'I vant to see the Guru.' So the guide takes her high up into the mountains, to a small village. At the village she says 'I vant to see the Guru.' They tell her she is fortunate. This is the Guru's village. But if she wants to talk to him, it will be very expensive and all she'll be able to do is say three words to him. She says 'I vant to see the Guru.' So they lead her to the Guru and tell her she can now say her three words. So she steps up to the Guru and says, 'Melvin, come home.'"

Everyone laughs in spite of their pain. Einstein, in particular, lets out his rich, warm belly laugh. But in his weakened condition it causes him to start coughing and gagging.

45

Einstein is sitting up in his hospital bed. His granddaughter Elsa is sitting on the bed beside him. He is reading to her from a big picture book of <u>Alice In Wonderland</u>.

"'I can't believe that!,' said Alice. 'Can't you?,' the Queen said in a pitying tone. 'Try again. Draw a long breath and shut your eyes.' Alice laughed. 'There's no use trying,' she said. 'One <u>can't</u> believe impossible things.' 'I daresay you haven't had much practice,' said the Queen. 'When I was your age, I always did it for half-an-hour a day. Why, sometimes I've believed as many as six impossible things before breakfast!'"

Elsa laughs. "That's funny, Grampa!"

Einstein laughs, too, delighted by Elsa's joy and amusement. Their happy moment together is cut short when a nurse enters the room.

"I'm afraid you're going to have to leave now, Elsa. Your grandfather needs to get some rest."

"I'm fine," protests Einstein.

"Doctor's orders, Professor."

"Very well." He turns to Elsa. "I'll see you later, okay?"

Elsa nods. "See you later, Grampa."

The Nurse escorts Elsa out of the room. Instead of lying down to get that rest the doctor ordered, Einstein grabs his notepad from the bedside table and proceeds to do some mathematical calculations. But after a few beats, he feels a twinge of chest pain. He gasps. Puts down the pencil. Catches his breath.

"So close," Einstein sighs. "And so little time left."

Einstein pushes the tray table away, lowers the front of the bed to its full reclining position, and closes his eyes to get some sleep. He starts to dream.

**

Einstein stands on the hour hand of a huge clock face. The hour hand is pointing at the number 4. The minute hand is pointing at the number 10. The second hand can be seen in the distance, ticking loudly as it moves from second to second toward Einstein.

There is a man standing precariously on the second hand, trying to keep his balance. It's Wolfgang Pauli. He sees Einstein on the hour hand and calls out to him. "I figured it out, Albert! I figured out why Alpha equals 137! It's an exponential function of pi! It's…"

And then Pauli loses his balance! He falls off the second hand and off the edge of the clock face into the great black void below! Einstein recoils in horror as he hears Pauli's anguished scream fade into oblivion.

**

Einstein wakes up from his dream. A chilling look of horror is on his face. And then a thought occurs to him. He reaches for the hospital phone and dials "0".

"How may I help you?," the Operator asks.

"Room 137 please."

Einstein waits impatiently for several seconds. And then the Operator comes back on the line.

"I'm sorry, Professor Einstein. I can't put you through to Professor Pauli… He just passed away. A heart attack…"

The phone drops out of Einstein's hand and tumbles to the floor. His expression is a combination of shock, confusion, and sorrow.

46

It's a few days later. Einstein is again sitting up in bed, working on his calculations, mumbling to himself as he does so.

"… 'an exponential function of pi'… that's what Wolfgang said in the dream… but what exponent? It could be anything!"

Einstein contemplates. Then he continues thinking out loud. "The hands of the clock were on the ten and the four. Ten to four." He thinks some more. "Ten to four… That's three-fifty…" And then it hits him.

"<u>Of course</u>! The cube root of 137 is a logarithmic function of pi to the fifth power! That's it! The last missing piece, by God! <u>The last missing piece</u>!"

Einstein is overjoyed. 36 years of mathematical confusion and frustration has finally ended!

**

Helen enters Einstein's hospital room. She is immediately struck by the change in Einstein's demeanor. He's grinning like the Cheshire Cat in <u>Alice In Wonderland</u>. His eyes are twinkling with mischievous delight.

"What is it, Albert? What's happened?" And then she realizes. "You did it?! You figured out the Unified Field Theory?!!"

Einstein nods. Helen gives him a big hug. "I'm so happy for you, Albert! My God, what an incredible achievement! You must be overwhelmed with joy! You..."

Helen has stopped talking because she has just seen the grin evaporate from Einstein's face. When she turns around to see what it is that has captured his attention and spoiled his mood, she discovers Chancellor Smith standing in the doorway.

"Congratulations, Albert," he says.

"Thank you," Einstein responds curtly.

"Shall I prepare a formal announcement?"

"I really couldn't care less what you do." He pauses. "With one exception."

"Oh really? What's that?"

"After I'm dead, don't pester Helen for my research notes. She'll put everything in order and get them to you in due time."

"That's fine. I have no problem with that."

"Good."

The tension between them is broken when an excited and exuberant Bertrand Russell suddenly barges into the room with a manuscript clutched in his hand.

"I've completed the Pacifist Manifesto, Albert!"

47

Bertrand Russell finishes reading from his manuscript as Einstein, Helen, and Chancellor Smith listen:

"People seek to minimize the danger of war by limitation of armaments. This is <u>not</u> the answer. Only the <u>absolute repudiation</u> of armaments and war can save us from universal death." He pauses. "Peace <u>cannot</u> be kept by force. It can only be achieved by understanding. We, therefore, appeal, as human beings, to human beings: Remember your humanity and forget the rest."

Bertrand Russell puts down the manuscript. Both Einstein and Helen are deeply moved by it.

"You did a fine job, Bertrand. A fine job," Einstein exclaims.

Einstein glances over at Chancellor Smith, who is having difficulty hiding his displeasure. After all, the Pacifist Manifesto reflects the antithesis of his political beliefs.

This is not lost on Einstein. In fact, hearing the Manifesto, and then seeing Chancellor Smith's reaction to it, enables Einstein to appreciate more clearly than ever before that Chancellor Smith is the epitome of the scientist/bureau-crat/warmonger that Einstein detests and that the Pacifist Manifesto has been written in opposition to. This leads Einstein to a final realization.

"I've changed my mind, Helen. I'm not going to reveal my discovery to the world."

Chancellor Smith is astonished and outraged. "<u>What</u>?!"

119

"I want you to destroy all my notes on the Unified Field Theory, Helen."

"You can't do that!," Chancellor Smith barks at Einstein.

"Don't tell me what I can't do!"

Chancellor Smith looks like he's going to have an apoplectic fit. He turns on his heels and storms out of the room.

Helen turns to Einstein. "Why, Albert?"

"The world is filled with two much fear and hate. Mankind needs to evolve humanistically before it gets any more technological power. Otherwise, that power is sure to be misused."

"I don't understand you, Albert. I thought you had decided that the discovery of truth is valid and worthy, <u>regardless</u> of how that truth might be used."

"Yes. I decided that. And I still believe it, which is why I no longer feel guilty about my Theory of Relativity. However, in my need to complete the Unified Field Theory, I forgot another important ideal which I once championed, one that I realize more than ever transcends all others. And that's responsibility." He pauses a moment. "Humanity is everyone's responsibility. Humanity must come first. <u>That</u> is the <u>absolute</u> and <u>ultimate</u> truth."

Helen shakes her head. "All those years of struggling for the answer…"

Einstein nods. "For years my guilt kept the answer from me. And now, having finally resolved that guilt and having come up with the answer, I purposely choose to withhold it from the world. It is ironic, isn't it?"

"Some people will think you died a pathetic fool."

"Let them," Einstein says with a gentle smile. "This isn't about ego, fame or glory. It's about responsibility. It's about doing the right thing. Not that revealing the Unified Field Theory would be the wrong thing. It's just that <u>not</u> revealing it is the better choice at this point in time, which makes it the right thing for me to do."

He pauses. "Maybe fifty years from now when someone else comes up with the answer, people will be more loving toward each other and use it for the ultimate good."

Helen looks lovingly at Einstein for a moment. "You're an incredible human being, Albert Einstein."

"Thank you, Helen."

Helen leans into Einstein. Kisses him gently on the lips. Then puts her arms around him and hugs him dearly.

"I love you, Albert," she says with tears in her eyes.

"And I love you."

48

Chancellor Smith is supervising several security guards who are boxing up Einstein's notes and carting them out of the office. Helen enters, shocked to see what is going on.

"What in God's name are you doing?!," she shouts at Chancellor Smith.

"What does it look like I'm doing?"

"You can't do this! Those notes are Albert's private property!"

"I'm afraid not. His research was paid for and belongs to Princeton University. And if you don't believe me, take a look at this."

Chancellor Smith removes an envelope from his coat pocket and hands it to Helen. "A court order allowing us to remove the notes from these premises."

**

Einstein is lying in bed. He looks pale and weak. Helen is standing beside him, telling him the news. "There's nothing we can do, Albert! He's got the notes and there's nothing we can do!"

One would expect Einstein to react with anger or sadness or some other appropriate emotion. But instead, he chuckles.

"Those notes will do him no good."

"What do you mean? I don't understand?"

"Those notebooks represent 36 years of failed attempts, flawed research, mistakes and misconceptions. They're as worthless to anyone else as they were to me. The only notebooks that are relevant are the ones I've been working on for the past several weeks."

"Where are they?"

Einstein reaches under his pillow and pulls out two notebooks. He hands them to Helen.

"There's one more thing, Helen," he says to her.

"What's that, Albert?"

"Don't let them turn the house into a museum."

49

Helen is building a fire in the fireplace in the living room of Einstein's house. Jung, Hans Albert, and Elsa are sitting on the sofa.

Hans Albert takes a very old, worn sheet of paper out of his pocket. "Dad wrote this on the day I was born." He reads from the paper. "'If others often plague thee, and do or say evil of thee, think also they came here without having asked for it. Think, though you may not like it – you, too, plagued others often. As this cannot be altered, think gently of everyone.'"

Hans Albert looks up, teary-eyed. After a few moments, Helen stands up and turns to the group. "Is everybody ready?"

They all nod. Helen takes Einstein's two notebooks and solemnly places them on the blazing fire. As the group watches the flames engulf the notebooks, each person's face reflects the loving thoughts of Einstein that they hold in their hearts.

After a few moments, the doorbell rings. Helen moves to the door, opens it, and finds Chancellor Smith standing before her with a stern and angry expression on his face.

"Where are the missing notebooks, Helen?," he confronts her.

"You're too late, Chancellor."

She steps aside so that Chancellor Smith can see the blazing fire.

Chancellor Smith is furious. "You <u>fool</u>! Do you realize what you've done?!"

Helen smiles. "I do, Chancellor. Indeed I do."

And without another word, she closes the door in his face and returns to the group in front of the fireplace to watch the flames as they take Einstein's Unified Field Theory to its fiery grave.

**

Einstein is on his deathbed in his hospital room. A nurse stands over him. She wipes a towel across his forehead. His face reflects the inner peace and contentment that he has finally achieved. He motions to the nurse to come closer. When she does, he whispers in her ear, "Remember your humanity... Forget the rest."

The nurse is overcome with emotion as she watches Einstein's eyes close for the last time.

THE END

www.ingramcontent.com/pod-product-compliance
Lightning Source LLC
Chambersburg PA
CBHW060632130626
46555CB00002B/774

* 9 7 8 0 6 1 5 7 7 3 8 1 0 *